Ramshackle Rose

Cathy Marie Hake

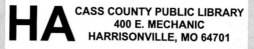

Heartsong Presents

To my dear friends,
Sulynn Means and Cathy Laws—
I've known you for ages.
You give of yourselves unstintingly,
and love with nothing less than your whole hearts.

A note from the Author:
I love to hear from my readers! You may correspond with me by writing:

Cathy Marie Hake
Author Relations
PO Box 719
Uhrichsville, OH 44683

ISBN 1-59310-924-6

RAMSHACKLE ROSE

one

Rose Masterson knelt by her picket fence and carefully culled a few more withering leaves. She stopped her tuneless humming as she got to her feet. For a moment, she wrinkled her nose at the way the white paint cracked and peeled on the slats of the fence that leaned inward toward her house. It would be lovely to paint the wood and brace it so it would stand upright like everyone else's did. . .but then, that would uproot the morning glory, and she couldn't bear to do that.

Turning her back on the fence, Rose started to hum again. She lifted a wicker basket and headed toward her cottage. Along the way, she picked some foxglove to give to Doc Rexfeld. He said it helped three of his patients who had heart palpitations, so Rose made sure she always kept some on hand. While she was at it, she cut some daisies and decided to drop them by Old Hannah's place.

Just before going inside, Rose lifted the hem of her striped, cream-and-olive washday dress and scraped the mud off her high-top, Vici kid, lace-up shoes. She ought to polish the durable, soft-as-glove leather, but that could wait until Saturday night so they'd look good for church.

"Miss Rose! Miss Rose!"

Rose turned and smiled at the freckle-faced towhead who stumbled up her brick path and stopped mere inches from

5

her. "Bless my soul! If it isn't Prentice, I'm not sure whom I'm looking at."

He giggled and opened his grubby hand. "Lookit! I lost two teeth!"

"Gracious! You're halfway to being a man already. I'll have to talk to your daddy about putting a brick on your head to keep you from growing up so fast."

Prentice jigged from one foot to the other. "Iff'n you tell him I'm that growed up, p'rhaps he'll get me a pocketknife."

Rose set her basket aside and crouched down. It wasn't exactly a ladylike position, but it let her get close enough for Prentice to see her face a bit better. Walleyed and near-sighted to boot, the six year old missed much of what went on around him. Rose knew he'd settle down, if only she'd take a moment with him. She cupped her hand around his shoulder and carefully considered what she should say next.

"I really want a pocketknife," Prentice told her breathlessly. He stopped wiggling and gave her a toothless grin. "Lotsa boys got 'em."

"I suppose that's true."

"They can do stuff—whittle, carve—do all kinds of nifty stuff."

The image of Prentice clumsily slicing his fingers with a sharp blade made Rose shudder. Inspiration struck. "You're right about the other boys having knives, though I think most of the ones who do are a far sight older than you. Seems to me that's fine for them, but you. . ." She squeezed his shoulder. "You, Prentice, are an exceptional young man. It seems to me, you ought to think more along the lines of something a bit more extraordinary."

"What's 'strod'nairy?"

"Extraordinary means something different and wonderful."

He scratched his side and heaved a sigh. "I'm already different 'nuff. I wanna be like all of the guys at school."

"Prentice, God wants you to be the person He made. If you're busy trying to be like everyone else, who's going to do the job the Lord has in store for you?"

"D'ya really think Jesus has something for me to do? I'm ...different."

"Seems to me, God needs special people to do special jobs. Why don't you think about that for awhile?"

"I reckon I could." He tilted his head to the side and turned a bit so he could focus on her more easily. "Just seems a fellow could use a pocketknife to do 'strod'nairy things."

"I've seen men do extraordinary things with paintbrushes. In the right hands, any tool can be made to do beautiful things. The trick is, each person has to discover what the tool is that God has in mind for him."

He scratched his side and heaved a sigh. "Can't think of nothing like that. I figured a pocketknife does lotsa stuff, so maybe I'd get good at doing something."

"Hmm."

"You stitched up my pocket. I wouldn't lose a knife."

Rose gave him a quick hug. "Oh, Prentice, I'd rather stitch your pocket shut than to have you put a knife in it just yet. There are other things a fine boy like you ought to keep in his pocket."

"You got something in mind, don'tcha?"

"As a matter of fact, I do."

His little head wagged a bit from side to side as he tried to get a closer look at her. In his excitement, he could scarcely stay still. "You gonna tell me what?"

"Better than that." Rose playfully tapped the tip of his nose. "Come in and look at my catalogue with me. I'll show you!"

Prentice scrunched his freckled nose. "You mean, we'd send away, mail order?"

"Certainly. It makes it so much more fun. Each day, you get to wonder if it will come. Anticipation means waiting with excitement for something to happen. You'll get to anticipate your. . ." She paused for a moment, then said with hushed, drawn-out relish, "Harmonica."

"Harmonica? A harmonica!" Prentice tugged on her full leg-o'-mutton sleeve and confessed, "I don't know how to play one."

Rose nodded. "I know. That's what makes it even better. You'll come to my house every day, and you can learn in secret. It shouldn't take much time; then you'll be walking down the street, astonishing everyone with your grand talent."

"I'd leave it here?" His features fell for just a moment. "But I can come every day?"

"There might be a day every now and then when I'm not at home, but you know you are always welcome, Prentice. Why, you could come right after school."

"Hurrah! Will you have cookies sometimes?"

Rose laughed as she stood. "Of course I will."

"Won't it take forever for the harmonica to come?"

"Just about the time you decide it's never going to arrive, it comes. Besides, you'll need a tiny bit of time to start letting those new, grown-up teeth come in."

"Stinky Callahan tole me they're going to come in all buck-toothed."

"No one can foretell the future."

Prentice kicked a pebble and sent it skittering away. "He

said my teeth would be as crooked and ugly as your fence."

Rose sat on the stoop, and Prentice flopped down next to her. She slid her arm around his thin body, and he wiggled closer. From the way he dipped his head, she knew he was trying to hide the tears that threatened to fall. Rose threaded her fingers through his corn-silk hair.

"I could change my fence if I wanted to, Prentice. I could, but I won't. Weak and wobbly as it is, it does a very special job right now. When I think on that, it gives me joy. It makes my fence beautiful to me." She bowed her head and kissed his hair. "I don't care if your teeth come in straight as a row of soldiers or crooked as can be. As long as you smile at me, you'll be handsome."

His little arms wrapped around her knees. "You make me wanna smile, Miss Rose."

❧

Garret Diamond dusted the last shelf of canned goods and nodded to himself. His emporium already looked better. Then again, that wasn't saying much. When he'd bought it two weeks ago, the emporium qualified as the most pitiful business he'd ever seen. As Buttonhole's only mercantile, this place should have been a thriving concern; but between the lack of customers and the abysmal figures in the books, the place simply wasn't turning anything close to a profit.

Ever ready to tackle a challenge and wanting to put his mark on the world, Garret took ownership and promptly locked the doors upon the completion of the transaction three days ago. Since then, he'd scrubbed, dusted, swept, sorted, and ruthlessly cut his losses. A list of things to order that ran at least two sheets long sat on the counter each evening. A heap of things sat near the back door—items that were of inferior quality, badly outdated, spoiled, or even chewed on by mice. Tomorrow, he'd haul it all out to the dump. Come Friday, the wagons would arrive bearing his new merchandise.

The post office occupied a back corner of the mercantile. In fact, the small rent the post office paid and the fact that its customers would have to wander through the store influenced Garret's decision to buy this particular store. He and the gnarled old postmaster, Mr. Deeter, got along well.

Garret hefted a box of canning jars and hauled them to the back door. Carefully, he set it down next to a crate of sun-faded fabric. The lids on the jars bulged, warning him if he jostled them and the glass broke, he'd end up with a stinky, explosive mess. As he straightened, someone rapped smartly on the glass window of the storefront.

Wiping his hands and face clean with a damp cloth, Garret headed toward the waiting customer. He knew the Pinaud's Brilliantine in his hair must have attracted an appreciable layer of dust, but that simply couldn't be remedied. Hastily readjusting his leather work apron to disguise the streak of dirt over his heart, Garret decided this was all he could do for the moment. It wasn't the best first impression, but. . .

He opened the door and couldn't think of a word to say to the woman standing there.

She wore a worn-out, striped dress that might have been pulled from a missionary barrel. What could have passed as a becoming hairstyle that morning now featured a wheat-colored topknot that slid precariously off to the left and a good dozen wisps and coils corkscrewing around her face and neck. Midafternoon sun illuminated her from behind, making her hair glow like a golden halo. Her eyes were more green than gray—definitely her best feature. She held a little towheaded boy in front of herself.

"I'm sorry, Ma'am, but we're closed still. The mercantile will open for business again on Saturday."

"We've come just to visit the post office. Surely, we can purchase a few stamps and· mail a letter."

"Mr. Deeter is out to lunch." He couldn't very well send them away or leave them standing out in the sun, so Garret opened the door wide and gestured for them to enter. "You're welcome to wait a few moments if you'd like. Please watch your step. I'm rearranging things and trying to establish some order. Allow me to introduce myself. I'm Garret Diamond."

"It's a pleasure to meet you, Sir. I'm Rose Masterson. This is Prentice—"

"Man, oh, man!" The little boy gawked about. "It's all different in here!"

The woman kept her hands on the boy and looked up at Garret. "Indeed, it is, but the post office is still in the corner. Imagine how hard it would have been to move all of the metal mailboxes and counter!"

The little boy giggled. "And the bars on the window. Daddy let me pull on the bars on his window at the bank. No one could ever move a window made of bars."

"I'm sure you're right." Garret glanced about the store, then grinned apologetically back at the mother and son. "Mr. Deeter has the post office shipshape. Wish I could say the same thing about the rest of the place."

"Prentice, there are boxes on the floor in this aisle. Let's go around to the far wall. We can play a game of draughts while we wait."

Garret took a closer look and noticed the boy had a problem with his eyes. The woman managed to guide him around the dangers. "I could hold the letter for you and give it to Mr. Deeter when he returns."

She smiled. "Why, thank you. I'd appreciate that." She handed him the letter and reached into the pocket of her apron to find her money.

Garret frowned. Her letter was addressed to Sears, Roebuck, and Company in a flowing, elegant script.

"You mightn't need to order things, Ma'am. I have fresh stock arriving tomorrow. Saturday will be the grand opening."

"Thank you, but Prentice and I read all of the descriptions in the catalogue and decided on one particular item."

Not one to dissemble, Garret still felt it reasonable to state his case. "I realize the emporium has fallen into disrepair and may not have met your needs. Those times are past. I've bought the place and plan to make it a going concern and serve Buttonhole's every need. If the article you wish is of a personal nature, I guarantee I'm a man of discretion."

"I appreciate your assurances, Mr. Diamond. Prentice and I have made our choice."

He inclined his head. "As you will."

The little boy tugged on her skirts. "I'm not going to get to lick the stamp now, am I?"

"I suppose not."

Garret smiled at the boy's wide, toothless mouth. "Looks like you would have done a fine job. Not many teeth in the way of your tongue." He snapped his fingers. "You know, I think I remember having a stamp. Let me check."

A few minutes later, he found his Little Stamp Book. "Aha! Just as I recalled. I have one last first-class stamp."

"Thank you for checking." The woman handed him two battered pennies.

"I lost my teeth today." Prentice diligently licked the stamp and stuck it in the corner of the envelope. His mother had stooped to hold it for him, and Garret noted how she made subtle allowances for her boy's vision problems, yet honored his independence. Prentice had her light hair, but he otherwise must have taken after his father. His mother's features were too finely chiseled, her form far slighter in build.

"I've been busy, so I haven't had an opportunity to meet anyone in town yet. Where do you folks live, and what does your husband do?"

Prentice giggled. "Miss Rose doesn't have no husband."

"My apologies," Miss Masterson interjected in a laughter-filled voice as she straightened up. "I should have thought to be more forthright. I moved to Buttonhole two years ago and went through the same confusion, so I understand precisely what lies ahead for you. I'm a spinster and live down the street and around the corner."

"The house with the tip-tilty fence," Prentice added on.

"Prentice and his father live across the street from me. His father is Hugo Lassiter, the bank teller."

Garret nodded. Miss Masterson had done him the kindness of subtly letting it be known that Prentice had no mother. No doubt, she minded the boy. *Lucky kid. She has a ready smile and a gentle heart. Odd that she seems so blithe about being a spinster. Any other woman would be embarrassed or coy, but she seems content as can be.*

"We ought to leave and allow Mr. Diamond to get back to his tasks." Miss Masterson set the envelope by the postal window. She took hold of Prentice's hand.

"You promised I could see Tom."

"Yes, I did." She looked up at Garret and explained, "You have a mouser named Tom who likes to sleep under the backporch steps. Would you mind if we exited from the storeroom?"

"I'll need to assist you." Garret lifted Prentice onto his shoulders. "I have discards piled by the back door." He offered his arm to Miss Masterson and led her through his store.

She halted and gasped when they got past the curtain that led to the storeroom. "Mr. Diamond, surely you cannot mean to waste all of these things!"

"I'm not disposing of all of it. Much of it is out of season, so I'm hauling it up to the attic." He frowned at several bolts of fabric. "Between the sun and the mice, those yard goods are ruined. The lids are bulging on those jars, and I won't sell anything that I think is spoiled or might make a customer sicken."

Miss Masterson squeezed by him, opened the back door, and tugged Prentice free. She set him down and ordered, "Go see Tom Cat." After the boy left, she turned back. "Mr. Diamond, Cordelia Orrick is a widow with three little girls. She lives in the green cottage at the far east end of Main Street. If you cut the first few yards off of those bolts, the fading problem is gone, and Cordelia is resourceful enough to work around the other parts. I'm sure she'd find the flannel particularly useful. As for the jars—if you empty them, I'll wash them. They can be filled with soup for shut-ins."

Garret leaned against a shelf and looked at the piles of junk. "A widow shouldn't have to mess with mouse nibbles."

"Ruth and Naomi gleaned." She smiled. "I have no doubt they ran into a few field mice."

Garret frowned. "Sharing the field with mice is to be expected; sharing flannel isn't."

Miss Masterson let her gaze wander about the storeroom. "Cordelia is a hard worker. You said you have stock arriving on the morrow. I'm not one to tell you how to run your business, but I'm willing to mind her daughters for the day if it would help." Before he could reply, she sashayed out of his store and collected Prentice.

Garret watched Rose Masterson wander down the street. He had the odd feeling she was completely unaware she'd left home without a hat. She'd worn dainty lace gloves, but she had a smear across her apron that looked suspiciously like jam. It matched the level of Prentice's mouth, a fact that Garret found charming. If the rest of the town were half as delightful, he'd settle in quite happily.

two

"Your emporium looks wonderful, Mr. Diamond."

"Thank you, Miss Masterson." The store owner tucked a pencil behind his ear. "You deserve part of the credit for its condition. You recommended Mrs. Orrick and watched her daughters after school yesterday. She was a tremendous help. I doubt I'd have gotten everything ready in time without her assistance."

"I did nothing; Cordelia is industrious as a bee. Bee—oh, that reminds me. I need honey."

"I'll be happy to get some for you."

"Piffle. I'm going to enjoy wandering about. I'll discover where you're keeping it." Rose turned away and sauntered through the mercantile. She hadn't voiced empty praise. The place shone. In the two years she'd lived here, Buttonhole's only dry-goods store had been pathetically understocked and dingy. The change was startling.

Rose finished scanning all of the shelves and displays, then set her wicker basket on the counter. She'd purposefully waited until the end of the day. From the steady stream of folks who went by her street all day, she surmised the mercantile's opening had, indeed, been a grand one. Plenty of small tasks kept her busy, and she was just as glad to tend to them and avoid the crowds. "Since the store's been closed a few days, I guess most of the townsfolk were happy to come by."

"It's been a pleasure to meet my new neighbors." Garret

Diamond looked down at the meager contents of the basket she'd brought, then back at her. "Were there other things you required? I'm happy to deliver the order to your home so you don't have to carry it."

"You're so very kind to make the offer, but I have what I need."

He looked at the box of shredded and spindled wheat breakfast biscuits. "I'm carrying a new product. It's a ready-made breakfast cereal with a far more pleasant flavor and texture. C. W. Post calls it Grape Nuts, but it's actually a wheat cereal, too."

"I already have Cream of Wheat at home, thank you."

He nodded. "I had some of that for my own breakfast this morning. I confess, I have a decided weakness for adding raisins to it."

Rose smiled and lifted the single banana out of her basket. "Brown sugar is my usual, but when they're available, I prefer sliced bananas in mine."

"Ah, and the very last one, I'm afraid. I'll be sure to keep them in stock. They've become quite the thing, haven't they?"

She set it down and remembered softly, "I had my very first one at the Philadelphia Centennial."

"I didn't have the pleasure of going to the centennial, but I went to the Chicago World's Fair. I count it one of the great adventures of my life."

"Oh, my! Did you ride on the Ferris wheel?"

He nodded. "Fifty cents to rotate on it twice. A shameful extravagance, but I don't regret it at all." He patted the counter next to her banana. "But I didn't have one of these there. Did you see the oranges I have in the crate over by the apples?

They're fresh from California. Train brought them straight through."

"I'm sure they're pure extravagances, too, Mr. Diamond, but my own trees are laden with a variety of other fruits, and I'm already going to be busy trying to preserve their bounty."

He propped both elbows on the counter and leaned toward her. "Perhaps I could tempt you to buy some sugar, paraffin, or canning jars?"

Rose burst out laughing. "I suppose I could use a loaf of sugar."

"Ah, but I don't just carry loaf or cone sugar, Miss Masterson. I have granulated sugar by the bag—so much more convenient, don't you think?"

"Buttonhole is going to be spoiled by the fancy goods you're importing."

He winked. "I certainly hope so. The sacks it comes in are double thickness, so you'll end up with a useful swatch of fabric."

Lula Mae Evert had toddled over to hear about the sugar. She reached up to primp her mousy brown marcel waves into place, then patted Rose on the arm. "Useful. Now there's a clever salesman. He already figured out the perfect word to hook you into making a purchase." She turned her attention to the storekeeper. "Rose, you'll soon discover, is the most practical woman the dear Lord ever created."

"Now that is high praise, indeed."

Rose felt a flush of warmth over those words, because that closely matched her prayer. Each morning, she asked the Lord, "Make me a blessing to someone in Your name today." It wasn't pride—it was her calling. God had been faithful in opening her eyes to places where she could be His servant.

"Five pounds or ten of that sugar, Miss Masterson?"

The man had an almost playful air about him that could charm even the grumpiest old crone. Rose drummed her fingers on the counter. "Why, Mr. Diamond, I'm shocked. You don't have it in twenty-five-pound sacks?"

"I do, but I'm afraid if I tried to sell it to you, picnic ants might carry you off."

She smiled at the outrageous picture his words painted. "Very well. I'll take ten pounds since I'm starting to can fruits. If you have any more of the bags with the tulips on them like you sold to Mrs. Sowell, I'd like that print, please."

It didn't take Mr. Diamond long to tally up her order. The man was quick with ciphering but accurate. He settled each item back into her wicker basket with care to keep it balanced—something most men wouldn't have thought to do. Rose tucked that fact away in the back of her mind. Mr. Diamond was not only clever and conscientious, he was also thoughtful.

As if he could tell what she'd been thinking, he turned the basket toward her and pushed the sugar off to the side. "I'll bring that sugar by after closing. It's too heavy for a lovely lady to carry."

Lula Mae Evert giggled. "Rose is strong as an ox, Mr. Diamond."

Rose gave him exact change and lifted her basket, then hefted the ten-pound bag of sugar—in the tulip print, as requested. "I'm quite capable. I thank you for your offer. I do hope many of your customers have thought to extend an invitation to church tomorrow."

"A few have."

Lula Mae lit up like a Fourth of July sparkler. "Well, of course you'll come, Mr. Diamond. Afterward, you just march right on over to my house. We're having pot roast, and I insist you share it."

"I'm afraid I'll have to turn down your kind invitation, Mrs. Evert. I'm going to Sunday supper at the reverend's."

Rose headed out the door and dipped her head just a shade so no one could see the smile tugging at the corners of her mouth. Gossip swept through Buttonhole at hurricane speed. The moment someone learned that the new owner of the emporium was a bachelor, every last mama with a marriageable daughter revised the Sunday supper menu, thus providing a dandy excuse to visit the store today. Lula Mae would mope all week for having missed this opportunity to snap up a fine young man for her daughter, Patience. By showing up so late in the day, she'd given all of the other mamas and daughters a head start at trying to attain the attentions of the charming—and probably richest—eligible man who'd just moved to town.

Oh, and if things went as Rose suspected, the matchmaking was going to turn into quite a show. Handsome Mr. Diamond would be in church tomorrow, but if any of a dozen young ladies had her way, he'd be at the altar for an entirely different reason within the season. Poor Mr. Diamond.

❧

Mrs. Evert watched Rose Masterson leave, then murmured, "Bless her heart."

Garret knew full well those three fateful words were a Southern belle's stock phrase for jumping in and dishing out gossip. He wasn't one to tolerate talebearing, even if it came wrapped up in pretty words or under the guise of news.

"She's just as sweet as that sugar you sold her."

"What a kind thing to say." Garret felt a twinge for having misjudged the woman.

She fussed with the large jet button at her throat. "Well, I'm only speaking the gospel truth. Rose Masterson is a dear, *dear* woman. She's different, you understand." The woman's voice dropped. "We all make allowances for her. Somewhere along the way, her parents failed her miserably."

"I though it Miss Masterson just said she'd only been living in Buttonhole a short time." Garret had the feeling if anyone needed allowances to be made, it was more likely Mrs. Evert. She wasn't making sense. "You knew her parents?"

"Of course, I didn't know her parents. They're dead, young man. She's an orphan."

"Such a shame. It's a good thing they reared her to be so capable and independent, though."

Mrs. Evert ignored every word he said and babbled on. "They went on to the hereafter due to the same tragedy, so she lost them both at once. Terrible as it is that she was left alone to fend for herself—they left her virtually penniless, too. She ekes by in that little house of hers and declares she'll never marry. Have you ever heard of such nonsense? Well, at first, we all assumed she was heartbroken from her loss; but she's never snapped out of her strange notion. She wouldn't do a body harm—so you needn't ever fret yourself over that. The woman's a glowing example of Christian charity. It's just that she's. . .well, dotty."

The minute Mrs. Evert paused to draw in a breath, Garret cut in so she'd cease the talebearing. "It's always a pleasure to learn a sister in the Lord is gifted with such charity. Was there anything else you'd like to buy, Ma'am?"

The remainder of the day flew by. Garret finally swept up, locked the front door, and counted out the till. Business had boomed today, but that could be attributed to curiosity and the fact that he'd kept the store shut for almost a week. Of course, the volume of customers was astronomical. Sales showed it, too. He'd turned a tidy profit. Good thing he'd filled the storeroom and had another shipment of goods due in on Monday.

It didn't take long to fill out his account book, but Garret had always found working with numbers quite easy. Organization was the key. He kept the financial ledger, then a record book for stock on hand and what he'd ordered. In a matter of a few months, he'd have a fair notion of the volume sold on average of each item, so he could keep his store stocked appropriately.

Garret knelt behind the counter, removed the secret panel he'd installed, and opened the lock on the Gruberman and Sons wall safe. He'd need to make a bank deposit on Monday. For now, he'd keep his funds secured here. He set them inside but kept out his tithe and offering for tomorrow. Once the secret panel clicked back in place, Garret stood and stretched. It had been a long day.

For the next hour, he restocked his shelves. Funny, how he'd learned so much about his neighbors by what they bought. Lumbago salve, Belgian lace, paregoric, and a Bailey teething disc—Garret had a glimpse of the town and its individual inhabitants.

And Rose Masterson—what did her purchases tell him? He turned a jar of honey so the label faced the front. She'd bought only necessities. Staples. No frills—nothing but the basics. Even if he'd had several bananas, would she have bought more than just that one? For all of the customers he'd had throughout the day, he could still recall each of the items that barely filled the bottom of Miss

Masterson's basket: honey, a single banana, cereal, yeast, one can of Borden's condensed milk, and half a pound of lentils. Oh—and the bag of sugar. Mrs. Evert's comments led Garret to believe Rose didn't have any leeway in her budget. He hoped he hadn't embarrassed the young lady by suggesting purchases she couldn't afford.

If Miss Masterson suffered a pinching purse, why had she recommended he ask Cordelia Orrick to assist him with the store? As it was, he'd already arranged with Mrs. Orrick to come dust and mind the store for a few hours a week. Depending on how the store did, Garret figured he could probably also hire Rose Masterson. The Lord instructed His sons to mind the widows and orphans, didn't He?

The lamplighter passed by, singing as he lit the fixtures along the way. The man had a pleasant baritone. Who was it that said she was his sister-in-law? The sparrowlike woman with the two hip-high sons who nearly danced a jig when Garret offered them each a sour ball—Mrs. S—it started with an S. Sowell—that was it. Garret smiled to himself. He wanted to put names and faces together as rapidly as he could. Miss Masterson was right about the confusion of meeting so many new people at once.

Rose. The name suited her. Oh, she wasn't a hothouse rose. If anything, she was a wild rose—a hearty yellow one with a fair share of thorns and a heady fragrance. Between watching the Widow Orrick's daughters and Prentice, she seemed to collect children about her. This Rose, no doubt, would have a handful of crickets and ladybugs about her. Garret shook his head. Normally not given to fanciful thoughts, he chalked up that whole vision as one triggered by overwork and exhaustion.

He turned off the light and headed up the stairs to his living quarters. He'd no more than made it up a few of the risers when a knock sounded on the store's door.

three

Rose shoved an errant curl back from her forehead and tried her best to ignore the mosquito bite on her right shin. The more she tried to forget that silly irritation, the more it itched. She'd dabbed camphor on it earlier today and gotten some relief, but her petticoats must have rubbed off the cure. Then again, the benefit of wearing long skirts was that she could balance on her right foot and use her left heel to—

Fingertips resting on the building, Rose nearly tumbled into the emporium when Mr. Diamond abruptly opened the door. "Mercy me!" she exclaimed.

His strong hand caught her arm and righted her. "Miss Masterson, are you all right?"

"Yes." She could feel the warmth clear through the wool of her cape and the serge of her gray dress. She couldn't very well explain what she had been up to. No lady confessed to scratching as if she were a mangy pup, and she certainly didn't refer to her limbs in the presence of a man. "Thank you. I momentarily lost my balance."

"It's my fault. I need to sand the step. It's a tad rough, and I can't have any of my customers tripping. Are you sure you're not hurt?"

"I'm fine. Just fine. You've had a busy day. I thought you might be tired. Here." She stooped and lifted a basket, then shoved it into his hands.

"What is this?"

"Just a warm supper. I doubted you'd feel much like cooking anything after working so long and hard." She flashed him a smile. "The jar ought to look familiar enough. It's one of your own."

He lifted the blue gingham cloth and smiled. Rose was glad she'd decided to bring by the simple meal, after all. It didn't take any longer to make a big pot of chicken stew and a large pan of corn bread than it did to make small ones for herself.

Mr. Diamond closed his eyes for a second and inhaled. "This smells great. I'm hungry enough to eat the basket, too."

"I slipped a pair of peach tarts under the corn bread, thinking you could have one for dessert and the other for breakfast. If you're that hungry, you could eat them both tonight. I hope you enjoy your meal." She stooped again and lifted her other basket.

"I will. But wait—what is that?"

"Oh—this is for Mrs. Kiersty. Bless her heart, she's down with a terrible case of quinsy. Soup and tea are about all she can tolerate."

"I'm sorry to hear that."

"Doc Rexfeld started her on slippery elm lozenges, and that honey I bought from you today ought to be quite soothing, too, don't you think?"

Garret looked into her eyes and nodded. "I'm sure the honey will be helpful. I recall using honey and lemon for coughs and sore throats. Permit me to send along a lemon."

Her lips parted in surprise but quickly lifted into a smile. "Oh, that would be so kind. I'm sure she'd appreciate your generosity."

He left the store's door wide open and set his supper basket on the counter. "It'll only take me a second." The fruit display to the left of the register held a full complement of choices. Rose watched the storekeeper ripple his long fingers over the fruit to select the lemon. He returned to the door. "Here you go."

"Thank you, Mr. Diamond." She accepted the fragrant lemon, slipped it under the cloth and into the basket, and turned to leave.

"Wait. You shouldn't be wandering alone in the dark. Let me escort you to her place and back home."

Rose gave him a startled look. "The lamps are lit, and Buttonhole is safe as a sanctuary. You're kind, but your worry is needless. God bless you, Mr. Diamond."

"God bless you, too, Miss Masterson."

She made it all of three steps down the walk before he had hold of her arm. "Where does Mrs. Kersey live?"

"Kiersty. She's at the boardinghouse."

"Why doesn't the cook at the boardinghouse make her soup?"

"Mrs. Kiersty is the cook. I'm afraid the owner, Mr. Hepplewhite, is able to scramble eggs and sear meat, but that's about the full extent of his culinary skills."

Garret chuckled. "Add to those two skills the fact that I can make hot cereal and slap together a sandwich, and you have the full extent of my kitchen expertise."

"Ah, but you can always open up a jar or can of something."

"Eating into my profits, eh?" He swiped the basket from her. "I confess, I've had the Hormel canned meat. Smoked oysters and tinned sardines aren't too bad. Tonight, I strongly considered celebrating by sitting down with a box of Cracker Jack."

Rose stopped beneath the lamppost and gawked at him. "Mr. Diamond, you cannot be serious!"

"Truth is the truth. You're right. After such a busy day, I was far too tired to bother cooking." He hefted the basket. Jars clinked against one another. "This basket is far too heavy for you to carry. How much soup did you put in this?"

"Two jars. I also included some applesauce."

"I smell bread, though."

"Yes, well, Mr. Hepplewhite and the others need bread. There are a few loaves for them."

Garret stared at her for a long moment, then quietly stated, "I'll bring flour, yeast, and eggs to you tomorrow."

"There's no need—"

"I agree," he interrupted smoothly. "There's absolutely no need for you to do the labor and supply the ingredients. I'm new here, but I aim to be part of the community. You wouldn't want to make me feel unwanted or unnecessary, would you?"

"Mr. Diamond, you've most assuredly chosen the profession best suited to your skills. I declare, I've never met a man who could find a bit of down fluff on a sleeve and sell the person a Christmas goose—at least, I never had until I met you."

His scowl looked anything but genuine. The glint in his hazel eyes and the lilt in his voice proved so. "Miss Masterson, I'm affronted by such an accusation. I'd never sell a customer a Christmas goose at this time of the year. Pillows would be far more suitable as replacements during spring-cleaning."

"Joel Creek's farm isn't far out of town. His wife tends to bring eggs, butter, and milk in once or twice a week, and she made a few superb pillows last year."

He held her arm as they stepped off the boardwalk and crossed the street. "You are a treasure trove of information,

Miss Masterson. I can see I'll need your assistance in getting to know everyone."

Rose didn't mind being friendly or making introductions, but if all Mr. Diamond wanted was to coax information out of her so he could sell things, he was barking up the wrong tree. But no—he'd just offered her staples so she could bake for their neighbors, and he'd wanted Mrs. Kiersty to have an expensive lemon to help her throat. Surely that proved him to be compassionate and concerned.

"I chose to open my store in Buttonhole because the town seems to have a gentle charm and caring about it."

She remembered aloud, "I came for the same reason. I visited several places before I decided to live here."

The jars clinked softly in cadence with his steps. "Meeting so many folk today confirmed my impression of how friendly everyone is. It heartens me to see how you're an integral member of the community after living here just a few years."

"Seeing the changes you've made and how you want to conduct a quality emporium, I can promise you, everyone is going to embrace your presence here. I daresay it took me almost a year to be regarded with the ease with which you've been welcomed."

"Why would that be?"

"I'm afraid they didn't quite know what to think of me. They eventually despaired of fitting me into a normal mold and decided I'm a bit dusty in the attic."

"Dusty in the attic?" He echoed her words with an equal measure of amusement to that which she'd instilled in them. "Just what is so dusty about your attic?"

"When I moved here, most of the gentlemen in Buttonhole felt I needed a man to tend my personal business, but I neither depend on nor answer to anyone except the Lord. Their wives and marriageable daughters felt I posed competition for the eligible young swains. It took them some time to realize none of that was true. Now, they accept me with genteel amusement. The fact is, I'm happy to be a spinster. The apostle Paul wrote about the ability of a single person to serve unhampered by marriage, and I find delight in doing just that. I confess, it's not the usual choice a woman makes, so they've decided I'm gently daft."

He pursed his lips and whistled a few notes. "Miss Masterson, as long as we're making confessions, I'm afraid I have one of my own to make."

"You do?" She stopped and looked at him.

The left side of his mouth kicked up in a rakish grin. "I'm just as dusty in the attic. At least, I plan to keep a very dusty attic for a few years."

Rose held her silence. She knew full well the mamas in the town were about to turn the table on this salesman. All day long, he'd charmed and convinced them to visit his store and tempted them to snap up what he offered. *Have you seen my wonderful. . . ? Wouldn't you like. . . ? It's perfectly suited to you. . .* Tomorrow, he'd be in church, where those selfsame women would have their daughters gussied up. *Have you seen my wonderful daughter? Wouldn't you like to sit with us? The church is lovely, isn't it? Perfectly suited for a beautiful wedding.*

"For shame, Miss Masterson."

Rose snapped out of her thoughts and gave him a startled look. "I beg your pardon?"

Mr. Diamond chuckled. "I hoped you'd be a kindred spirit and accept me as a man who needs to establish his business before he could devote himself to one of the local ladies and start a family. I can see you've already cast me to the vagaries of the matchmakers and consider my cause lost."

"I know the matchmakers."

"Ah, but you don't know me." He took her arm again and steered her toward the boardinghouse. "Suffice it to say, I'm about to confound Buttonhole's citizens by failing to fall madly in love with one of the fair maidens."

"Do you read much, Sir?"

"It's among my favorite pastimes."

"Perhaps it's best if I just quote from Robert Burns. 'The best-laid plans of mice and men oft go astray.'"

He opened the door, and his breath washed over her as he dipped his head and added in a tone only she could hear, "Don't stop there. 'And leave us naught but grief and pain/For promised joy.' I'm not about to be ensnared by the plans and promises of others. I've plenty of plans for myself."

❧

Punctuality, for being a virtue, should carry with it some level of protection. The wry thought made Garret smile as he wiped the last dab of shaving lather from his chin. He'd determined to show up on the church steps just two slim minutes before the service began. After worship, he'd gladly greet his new neighbors, then make his excuses and go to the parsonage to dine with the minister and his wife.

Garret had concentrated his attention on setting up the store, and he'd been so busy with the grand opening, he'd failed to see the obvious. Rose Masterson did him a great favor by letting him know he was considered eminently eligible. Or was that imminently?

He'd awakened this morning with a plan in place—he'd

keep a friendly distance and let the good parson and his wife spread the message that Garret Diamond couldn't commit himself to a bride until he'd established himself.

Oh, he'd certainly not mind meeting the young ladies who were prospective bridal candidates. It would be wise to get to know them, learn of their temperaments, personalities, and quirks. Rushing recklessly into marriage simply wouldn't do. If he kept a slight distance at the start, it would permit him to meet the full selection instead of misleading one particular young lady into thinking he'd been smitten by love at first sight. It wasn't right to dally with a girl's heart, and since he had to wait to marry until his business flourished, it was essential to make his decided lack of romantic intentions quite clear from the start.

When the time came, he wanted a woman who would be his helpmeet in the fullest sense of the word—to help with the store, to be a loving wife and a good mother. Hard working. Sweet spirited. Caring. Virtuous.

Caring and virtuous. . . He thought of Miss Masterson. She hadn't bought the honey for herself. It wasn't expensive in the least, but if Miss Masterson's finances were half as strained as Mrs. Evert claimed, her small sacrifice of giving that jar to Mrs. Kiersty was akin to the widow in the parable who tithed her last mite. When he delivered the flour, butter, yeast, and eggs he'd promised, Garret would slip in a jar of honey for her to keep for herself.

With that decision made, Garret smiled at himself in the small mirror over the sink. He purposefully avoided splashing on his customary bay rum, snapped his elastic suspenders in place over a spanking new French percale shirt, and secured a turn-downed collar he'd saved for today. He felt a momentary twinge of homesickness. Great-aunt Brigit knew just the right amount of starch to use.

The school bell pealed. Parson Jeffrey had mentioned the church didn't have a bell yet, so they used the school's bell as a call to worship. Half an hour ago, it rang twice. Now, it rang thrice. Ten minutes until the service. Garret donned a subtle charcoal-and-black vest, grabbed his suit coat and hat, and went downstairs. He allowed himself a few minutes to eat a shiny red apple before he stepped out his door. . .and into a sea of pastels and foamy lace.

four

"Good morning!" a chorus of sopranos sang out.

"No better way to start the day than with worship." He shut the door to the mercantile and removed his hat. A gentleman didn't keep his hat on in the presence of ladies. It also gave him something to do with his hands. "I'm sure the preacher has a good message for us today."

"You won't hear a word of it if these gals won't stop flocking and clucking like hens." A spry old man hobbled through the bustled dresses and batted away a few feathers arcing from Sunday-best hats. He extended his hand. "I'm Zeb Hepplewhite, owner of the boardinghouse, and I'm invitin' you to come sit by me on the bachelor bench."

Garret had no idea what the bachelor bench was, but from a few crestfallen sounds the girls around him made, he surmised he'd just been tossed a rope. He shook Zeb's hand as if it were a lifeline. "Pleasure to meet you, Hepplewhite. I'd be honored to join you."

Once seated in church, Zeb rumbled, "This back bench is bachelor territory. Back bench t'other side's for the mamas with crybabies. Front pew on the left is for the parson's family, and front pew on the right is courtin' row. A buck sits there with a gal, and the good folks of Buttonhole take it to be a declaration of intentions."

Garret nodded his understanding as he looked at the rows of oak pews that lined the boxy white church. "Thanks," he said in a low tone. "I might have blundered badly."

Zeb opened his hymnal and covered his chuckle with a rusty cough. "Wouldn't be the first person to. Miss Rose sat here on the bachelor bench the very first Sunday after she moved to town. As it turns out, 'twas a fitting choice. Oliver Sneedly told her she was in the wrong place, so she scooted across the aisle. Was a few months afore the folks hereabouts stopped squawking and let her be. She has a knack of taking a fussy babe and hushing it."

As the congregation stood to sing the first hymn, Rose Masterson slipped into the crybaby pew. Garret had seen her three times by now, but this was the first time he caught sight of Miss Rose when she'd bothered to tend to her appearance. She made for quite an eyeful. Tamed coils of golden hair framed her face and peeped out beneath a sensible black straw hat trimmed with a minimum of folderol. The midnight blue silk military loop and hooks on her snowy bodice might have looked mannish on someone else, but the way they graduated in size from her tiny, cinched waist up the front served to prove just how feminine she could be. Her deep blue skirt draped over a very modest bustle, giving her a silhouette any man would find admirable. Then, her head turned.

She had a smudge of white on her right cheek.

Rose didn't have a vain bone in her body. If he were a gambling man, Garret would bet his bottom dollar it wasn't powder on her cheek. It had to be flour. He reached up and brushed his own cheekbone in a silent message.

She didn't understand.

"Flour," he mouthed silently.

Any other woman in the world would have been mortified.

Rose's eyes lit with appreciation, and she swiftly rubbed away the white with her gloved hand as she sang every verse and the chorus of "Come, Thou Fount of Every Blessing" by memory. She looked back at him, her brows raised in silent query.

Garret nodded and grinned. She'd erased the evidence of her baking, at least from her face. As she lowered her gloved hand, the flour made a faint swipe on the side of her dark skirt.

By the time Parson Jeffrey finished an excellent sermon on living by faith and the congregation stood to sing the benediction, Rose held a sleeping baby in each arm. Instead of her full sleeves ballooning out as fashion dictated, they both caved in. The knot in the uppermost military cord loop was soggy from having become a teething chew. A suspicious damp spot marred her skirt, yet she wore a look of utter contentment.

The Scripture of the day from the third chapter of 1 John ran through his mind again. *"My little children, let us not love in word, neither in tongue; but in deed and in truth. And hereby we know that we are of the truth, and shall assure our hearts before him."*

Yes, he'd come to the right place. Good people—people like Rose Masterson—lived here.

❦

"King me!" Leigh Anne clapped her hands delightedly.

"Now weren't you clever." Rose slipped a draught atop one of Leigh Anne's red ones. They sat by the cracker barrel in Diamond Emporium and chattered as they played the game. Rose knew Leigh Anne's grandma timed her shopping to coordinate with the end of the school day, but she'd been a bit late today. It was too hard for Leigh Anne to walk about the store due to the heavy steel-and-leather leg braces she wore, so Rose challenged Leigh Anne to a game of draughts.

"I get a lot of practice at board games." Leigh Anne tried to be subtle as she scratched below her knee.

Rose knew the brace often rubbed, so she leaned across the board and whispered, "Do you need some salve?"

"I ran out," Leigh Anne admitted.

Garret sauntered over. He looked quite dashing in a casual sort of way. Instead of wearing a suit coat as he worked, he always wore a vest and gartered his shirtsleeves.

From the way the young girl blushed, Rose decided to say something so Garret wouldn't know what the conversation was about. Leigh Anne loathed her braces and would probably rather be shaved bald than to have them become a topic of conversation. Rose teased, "Seems to me you've said the same thing about root beer barrels in the past—that you've run out."

"Root beer barrels?" He squatted down beside Leigh Anne and studied the checkered board. "Looks like you have Miss Masterson on the run. Why don't you hand me one of those draughts you captured?"

Leigh Anne happily handed over one of the black wooden pieces.

Garret hefted it in his hand a few times, then stood. He grabbed a few root beer barrel candies and soon was juggling the draught amidst a flurry of candies. When he stopped with a flourish, he dumped the candies into Leigh Anne's lap. "Miss Masterson trounced me in a game a few days ago. From now on, any time you beat her, I'll pay you a piece of candy. We've got to stick together, you and I."

"I'll share with you, Miss Rose."

Rose shook her head. "No, Leigh Anne. You earned those candies."

"Grandma says a girl should only accept gifts and candy from a man if he's her beau. I can't have a beau."

"You are a bit young," Garret agreed.

Leigh Anne shook her head so vehemently, her dark brown curls swirled. "I'm almost fourteen. Gladys is twelve, and her initials are already carved in the sweetheart tree. No one will have me."

"Leigh Anne, you don't know that," her grandmother refuted, having just arrived. "God might have someone special just for you."

Hands knotted around the candies in her lap, Leigh Anne whispered, "I'm crippled."

Garret hooked his thumbs in his suspenders and scowled. "Miss Leigh Anne, your limbs might be on the weak side, but your mind's sharp as a tack, and your heart is sweet as honey. It occurs to me, one of these days, some smart fellow is going to count himself mighty lucky to have an excuse to sweep you into his arms and carry you about."

"You're so romantic, Mr. Diamond." Leigh Anne drew in a quick breath and blurted out, "Why aren't you married?"

"Leigh Anne!" Her grandmother pressed her hand to her bosom and nearly had apoplexy.

The door to the emporium opened, and as a couple of ladies entered, Garret nodded his greeting, then blithely turned back to Leigh Anne. "You're asking what everyone else is wondering. The truth is, a man has no right to call on a woman when he doesn't have the time to attend her. I need to build my business so I'll be able to provide well for a family. When the time comes, I want my emporium to be stable so I can dedicate myself to being a good husband, just as Christ cared for His bride, the church."

"Why, now, isn't that sensible of you?" Lula Mae Evert cooed as she came closer. "As busy as you've been, it should not take long at all for you to realize great success with your store."

"It's thriving. Everyone says so," Mrs. Busby agreed.

A little boy at her side tilted his head far back so he could look up at Garret. "Papa says you'll be ready to marry up by Christmas."

"Is that so?" Garret nearly choked on the root beer candy he'd popped into his mouth.

Rose stood and started smacking him between the shoulder blades.

"Yeah, to my cousin, Missy Pat—"

His mother's hand clapped over the boy's mouth. "We really must hurry. I just stopped in to buy. . ." Her voice died out, and her already-pink cheeks went positively scarlet.

"Some?" Garret recovered enough from his choking that he rasped out the prompt.

"Matches," Mrs. Busby said in a strangled tone.

Rose had to credit Garret. He resumed his professional demeanor and ignored what amounted to an embarrassing pun. He acted as if the simple request couldn't be interpreted in any other manner and nodded sagely. "Matches. Parlor, small box, or vest matches?"

"Mr. Busby doesn't smoke. I believe I'll take some for both kitchen and parlor."

Garret walked toward a nearby shelf, tapped the edge, then turned around. "Mrs. Busby, I know my predecessor sold lucifers, and I have the remaining stock on the shelf. Keeping them there goes against my grain. I'd far rather give you a flint striker than sell you these old-fashioned phosphorus lucifers. I don't think they're safe. I have Red Top matches due in later this week."

"Oh, la!" Mrs. Busby waved her hand dismissively. "I learned to cook and keep house with lucifers, and I've never once had a single spark go astray."

Mrs. Blanchard bobbed her head in agreement. "They're ever so much more convenient. Why, I simply keep a quart jar of water close by to douse the match when I'm done."

"I've seen too many sparks from those for my own comfort. I took to mail-ordering Red Tops a year ago," Rose said.

"As do I." Leigh Anne's grandmother put a can of Wedding Breakfast coffee on the counter. "Leigh Anne, are you and Rose about finished with your game?"

"About six more moves, Grandma."

"I'll be sure she gets home," Garret promised as he headed to the counter. Rose noted he'd not taken matches along with him for Mrs. Busby. Instead, he'd stubbornly taken along a striker. "I'll be sure to keep sulfur tops for you ladies. There's no reason for you to need to order such necessities by mail."

He tallied up everyone's purchases, sent them on their way, and Leigh Anne finished the last move of her victorious game. As Rose stood and shook the wrinkles out of her gown, the shop bell rang.

"Mr. Diamond, I'm going to have to throw myself at your mercy." Trevor Kendricks shuffled by the door. "Ma's under the weather and wants some embroidery stuff—*pink*." His face matched the color he requested.

"Embroidery floss. . ." Garret folded his arms across his chest. "I have it by the skeins, but I'm hopeless as can be when it comes to choosing a matching hue."

"Did she tell you a name or number?" Leigh Anne asked softly. "Corticelli numbers the spools."

"Can't rightly recollect. I get the numbers all squirreled up in my brainbox. I have a strand here in my pocket."

"While you youngsters match that up, I'm going to go ahead and buy a postage stamp." Rose went to the counter and slipped two cents to Mr. Deeter.

"Here you are, Rose." He slid the stamp to her and jerked his thumb back toward some brown-paper-wrapped packages on the counter. "You had more parcels come today, but they were too late, so Tommy will be delivering them tomorrow. If you needed either of these immediately, I thought you might want to know they're here."

Rose smiled. "Oh, I'll carry the smaller one home with me. I've been waiting for it."

Garret called over, "I'll be happy to carry the other box to your house after I close tonight."

"How very kind of you."

Mr. Deeter bobbed his head. "He's a good'un. Garret, you'd best come claim it now. I'm liable to lock up the post office while you're busy with customers, and I don't want Miss Rose to think we forgot about her parcel."

Garret strode over as Rose licked the stamp and applied it to the corner of the envelope.

Garret's features went taut, and Rose knew he'd read the address: Sears, Roebuck, and Company.

five

Rose swept up the smaller package. "Isn't this convenient? The post office and the mercantile working hand in hand. I declare, Mr. Diamond, you've made your emporium such a cheery place, it's a pleasure to stop in."

"Thank you." From the hectic blush on her cheeks and the way she suddenly plunged into chatter, he could tell she was embarrassed. She undoubtedly didn't want to hurt his feelings, but she'd grown accustomed to mail-order shopping. It might take a short time for her to change her ways. He could be understanding and bide his time. Garret decided to wait until he could speak with her privately. Though she expressed the firm wish to remain single, Miss Masterson's business was worth courting.

"We found it!" Leigh Anne called out.

"Wonderful." Garret hefted the larger box and carried it over to his work counter.

"And Leigh Anne shared her candy with me," Trevor said. He sounded like he had a marble in his mouth.

Garret turned so the youngsters couldn't see him and gave Rose an exaggerated wink. He went over to them, then praised, "That does look like a dandy match. Miss Leigh Anne, are you about ready to go home now?"

"Yes, Sir."

"I'm still trying to figure out where everyone lives."

"Oh, we're neighbors. Leigh Anne's two doors down from

me on Elm." Trevor handed the spool of embroidery floss to Garret and dug into his pocket. The penny he pulled out bore a fair coating of lint, which he rubbed at. "Sorry."

"Not a problem." Garret flipped the penny onto the counter and lifted Leigh Anne into his arms. "Miss Masterson, would you please mind the store for me for a few moments while I escort this pretty young lady home?"

"Now wait a minute." Trevor handed the floss to Leigh Anne. Her hand closed around it as her mouth formed a perfect O. The strapping teen grabbed the dainty girl from Garret.

"I'm happy to mind the store." Rose pulled an apron from a hook on the wall.

"Seems to me Mr. Diamond ought to mind his own store." Trevor's arms tightened. "Leigh's my neighbor. No use in him wandering around when I can take care of her far better."

"Miss Leigh Anne." Garret reached for her. "I promised your grandmother I'd be sure you got home."

"You're keeping your word. You can be sure I'll carry her home safe as can be. Leigh, hook your arm 'round my neck. We need to get going. Ma's wanting her floss, and you don't want your grandma fretting herself about you."

Rose tugged Leigh Anne's skirts down to keep her ankles covered. "Mr. Diamond, I can personally vouch for Trevor's character. He's dependable as the day is long and strong, as you can plainly see."

"Miss Leigh Anne." Garret beetled his brows and gave her a stern look. "If you aren't comfortable with this arrangement—"

Her arm wound around the lad's neck. "Miss Rose says it's acceptable. I think we're just fine. Thank you for asking, though."

Garret held the door, then shut it after they left. As he

turned around, Rose didn't bother to hide her smile. She shook her finger at him. "For shame, Mr. Diamond. You don't want anyone playing matchmaker on your behalf, and here you are, nocking an arrow on Cupid's bow for those two."

"Am I supposed to understand what you're talking about?" The deep creases bracketing the corners of his upturned mouth made it clear he knew precisely what he'd been doing, and his sudden ploy at innocence was just another game.

She took off the apron she'd donned and draped it over his shoulder. "I'll take that package with me now."

"Speaking of packages, Miss Masterson, you've gotten a total of three in the week since I've been here."

Rose's step faltered. *Please, Lord, don't let him ask me about it.*

❧

"I'm sorry the mercantile didn't meet your needs in the past and certainly hope you'll allow me the chance to carry the goods you need now that I've taken over."

Color stained her cheeks.

Garret felt like a cad. "I understand there are times when a lady might wish to purchase items of a personal nature through a mail-order catalogue. Please don't think me indelicate. My intent is to run a business where you are able to find any of your other needs."

"I've been here twice in the past week to purchase things. If you'll excuse me, I must go."

She swept out of the mercantile with equal amounts of speed and grace. Garret watched her go, then set about reworking the display of homeopathic curatives and medicaments. They were no more than a jumble of tins, bottles, and jars in a case he'd not yet reached. As he started to empty the case and examine the contents, he groaned. Most of the bottles contained spirits and unnamed ingredients. Two were so old, sludge had formed in the bottom. A jar of Vaseline, a tin of bag balm, and Red Clove liniment were all he salvaged. The rest, Garret dumped into a bucket. He'd ask Doc if any of them were worth keeping.

As he set the bucket in the storage room, Garret couldn't help thinking the woman on the jar of Magnificent Mane looked quite similar to Rose Masterson. She had the same delicate features, and he imagined when Rose unpinned her hair, it would be every bit as luxurious.

He shook his head. *I've seen several lovely girls today—all tidy as can be, who would do credit to any man they wed. Missy Patterson, Hattie Percopie, Anna Sneedly, Constance Blanchard. . . Each of them from fine family backgrounds, soft-spoken—and utterly boring. Rose—mussy little Rose who forgets her hat half the time, whose topknot skids around, whose sash is more likely to be mangled than tied in a pretty bow—she's the one I think of. What's come over me?*

He tilted his head and rubbed the back of his neck. The memory of her flowing script on that envelope addressed to the catalogue flashed through his mind.

Then and there, he determined he'd win her business—*all* of her business. He'd come to Buttonhole full of dreams of making his mark in the world. He didn't imagine himself as building a business empire. More than anything, he wanted to be a man who served the Lord and his fellowman. To his way of thinking, if every man loved his family and bettered his community, the world would be a far better place. Once he stabilized his emporium, Garret figured the Lord would send a wife his way. One step at a time—one foot in front of the other in a sure and steady walk.

He had no way of knowing what Miss Masterson ordered. Simply put, it stretched his imagination that she'd needed four different shipments of things of such private nature that she'd needed to mail-order them in such a short span of time.

On occasion, he'd even ordered from a catalogue or two himself. The catalogues always promised their prices were lower than those of local merchants—a fact that Garret felt was not borne out. Nonetheless, if Miss Masterson was barely eking by, she might well have been convinced by the catalogue that she'd be saving money by dealing with them. Garret decided he'd show her the truth by looking through the pages of the mail-order book and demonstrating that his prices were quite comparable. The convenience of having the purchases on hand rather than waiting for them and paying postage ought to tip the scales in her mind. After all, she did seem like a reasonable woman.

Indeed, she was a reasonable woman, and he was a rational man. With that level of practicality betwixt them, she'd come to see the light.

Garret wouldn't begrudge her a final item. In fact, he'd promised to personally deliver the two other boxes that had come for her. It would give him an excuse—no, he corrected himself—a *reason* to go speak to her this evening.

The store was a bit slow. Garret didn't want to pay a call in the rumpled shirt he'd worn all day, so he stuck an iron on the store's potbellied stove. Great-Aunt Brigit always made ironing look so simple. Garret realized the chore was far more complex than he'd imagined. He couldn't decide whether to start on the collar or the sleeves. He scowled at the shirt. *Or do I start in on the main part?*

He slung a shirt over the board and decided to proceed

from one side to the other. As soon as the flatiron heated up, he attacked. With more zeal than skill, he mowed over the buttons. Just then, he felt something underfoot. A quick downward glance revealed that one sleeve dragged on the floor. He flipped it up, then sniffed. Something smelled— "Oh no!" He jerked the flatiron off of the shirt and scowled at the arch-shaped, yellowbrown scorch marring the garment.

An hour later, the rest of the shirt looked passable. Garret covered up the damage with a vest and coat. He applied fresh pomade to his hair and decided to take along something to sweeten up the lady. The row of clear glass candy jars caught his attention.

Mints? No. She might think he was telling her she had bad breath. Sour balls? Garret shook his head. He didn't want her to misconstrue them into an odd symbol of him thinking she was tart-tongued. No man took chocolates to a woman unless he intended to court her, so he ruled those out at once. She hadn't wanted any of Leigh Anne's root beer barrels. Tootsie Rolls! Yes, that would be the ideal candy. It would be a subtle reminder to her that Diamond Emporium carried the finest, the latest, the best. It would also take a little while to eat, so that would stretch out the visit long enough to permit him sufficient time to state his case.

❧

"Just a few more, then I'll help you." Rose switched the cold flatiron for the hot one, then slid it over Hugo's worn blue chambray shirt. She'd mended it as best she could, but the garment wouldn't last much longer. Mary Ellen had sewed these very buttons on it the first time she and Rose shared a cup of tea. Now, that shirt was Hugo's favorite—a reminder of his dearly departed wife's devotion.

"D'ya really think I can do it?" Prentice's glasses bobbed upward as he scrunched his nose. "Lotsa folks say I'm clumsy."

"If you always bother to listen to bad opinions, you won't have time to live your life. I hold with the notion that it's far better to try and not quite get it perfect rather than to sit still and never see or do anything."

"That's why you're so fun."

"Why thank you, Prentice. I take that as quite a compliment."

Heavy footsteps sounded on the porch, and a few solid, thumping knocks announced the arrival of a man.

"C'mon in, Hugo!" Rose called as she brushed more water from the noodles she'd boiled a few hours earlier onto the placard of the shirt to starch it. Pressing the iron to the cloth, she detected the faint aroma of noodles rising in the steam. It sharpened her appetite.

"Dad's bringing wood." Prentice galloped over to the door when it didn't swing open. He jerked it open, then stammered, "Miss Rose, it's not my daddy."

six

Rose put the flatiron back onto the stove and glanced over her shoulder. "Mr. Diamond! Do come in."

"I have those other packages for you."

She scanned the room. "Oh, yes. Could I trouble you to place them over by the hall tree?"

"I'd be glad to."

"We already got our surprises in the mail today." Prentice eagerly followed behind the storekeeper.

Rose held up her forefinger. "But we both know it won't be a surprise if you tell anybody what it is."

Prentice jerked his hand out of his pocket.

"You may sneak past Mr. Diamond and go put your special thing beside mine in the drawer of the parlor desk."

"Yes'm, Miss Rose."

Garret straightened and watched the boy leave the room, then gave her ironing board an assessing look. He cleared his throat. "There you are. I'll be going now."

Slipping the shirt onto a hanger, Rose laughed. "If you don't mind me finishing Hugo's shirts, you're welcome to join us all for supper."

"I, uh. . .thanks, but —"

"Prentice and his father live across the street. We exchange favors. I do their laundry, and Hugo hauls wood for me and refills my stove and lamp gas. Since I need starch on laundry days, I usually make a noodle casserole. It's silly for me to

49

make one just for myself, so they always join me on washday for supper."

"That's quite an arrangement. Practical."

"It's sensible. The evening's still warm, and there isn't much of a breeze. Please feel free to remove your coat. Hugo always dines in his shirtsleeves."

Mr. Diamond's face went ruddy. He curled his fingers around his lapels and closed the distance between them. He looked down at her and lowered his voice. "Perhaps you could give me a bit of advice regarding laundry."

Rose felt a bit dizzy from his nearness. She busied herself arranging the last shirt on the ironing board and tried to sound casual. "Do you have a stubborn spot that won't wash out?"

"I haven't tried to wash it yet."

"That's probably a point in your favor. The wrong solution or temperature can set a stain. What is it?"

He let out a sigh and peeled out of his jacket. With a hooked thumb, he dragged the right side of his vest's neckline farther to the side of his chest.

"Oh, my. That's a nasty scorch." She looked up at him. "I take it you're unaccustomed to doing your own laundry?"

"Correct. I don't have the talent you're demonstrating at this moment. I looked away from the ironing board and failed to keep the iron in motion. Have I ruined the shirt?"

"Did it burn all of the way through, or is what I'm seeing the worst of the damage?"

"The very tip is darker."

"Daddy!"

Prentice's shout rescued Rose from gawking at Mr. Diamond. He'd continued to stand close enough that her skirt brushed his leg, and the line of the scorch arched right up toward his shoulder, accentuating the breadth of his shoulders. She'd almost reached up to touch the mark—just to check the severity of it, she hastened to tell herself. She cleared her throat and called out, "Hello, Hugo. Supper and your laundry are about ready."

Hugo dumped an armload of logs by the hearth, dusted off his hands, and mussed Prentice's hair. "Sounds great. Were you a good boy today?"

"Pretty good. I can't stand on my head yet. Miss Rose is going to help me learn how."

Suddenly, it all sounded wrong. Rose could only imagine what these men must be thinking—that she'd demonstrate for Prentice by upending herself in a completely undignified display of petticoats and limbs. She'd just told Prentice what others thought didn't matter, but she started reconsidering that statement. Hugo would surely understand, but how could she sit across the supper table from Mr. Diamond if he believed she'd—

"Miss Rose taught you how to ride a bicycle and walk on stilts," Hugo said smoothly. "It makes sense she'd be the one to show you that, too."

"I'm sure all it will take is for someone to stabilize Prentice," Rose murmured. "Hugo Lassiter, have you met Mr. Diamond, the new mercantile owner?"

Hugo walked over and shook Garret's hand. "So are you—oh. I did the same thing—scorched a shirt. Mine looked much worse. I came to Rose for help with that disaster. Though I'm sorry your shirt met the same fate, it's reassuring to learn I'm not the only man in town who botched up his shirt."

Garret's mouth twisted into a wry smile. "The only domestic skills I possess are sweeping and eating."

"So he's joining us for supper." Rose switched flatirons again and shoved a few curls away from her forehead with the back of her wrist. "Hugo, do you mind if he borrows one of your shirts so I can apply some peroxide to that scorch?"

"Not a bit."

Rose made sure she didn't offer the blue chambray. It didn't take but a few moments to pop an extra place setting on the table, and soon they all bowed their heads for grace.

"You'll never imagine what came on the train," Hugo said once they started eating. He didn't wait for anyone to actually guess. "A washing machine for Cordelia Orrick! Nice, big, modern one."

"You don't say!" Rose set down her glass.

"It's another one of those mystery gifts." Hugo mixed honey with his peas and used his knife to lift them to his mouth.

"Mystery gifts?"

"Yes, Mr. Diamond. It seems folks in Buttonhole look out for one another. Every so often, something someone needs just. . ." Rose spread her hands, palms upward. "Appears."

"Miss Masterson, are you telling me someone secretly bought the Widow Orrick a washing machine?"

"My daddy told you; she didn't." Prentice slurped some milk. "Ever'body else calls her Miss Rose. How come are you calling her Miss Masterson?"

"We've only recently met. It's mannerly to address one another that way. Miss Masterson deserves my respect."

Rose smiled at him and nodded her head. "That's most kind of you, but in truth, I'm of the opinion that respect is better shown than spoken of. We're all brothers and sisters in the family of God. I'd take no offense to you addressing me by my given name."

"Likewise."

Prentice squinted through his thick glasses. "Your name is Likewise?"

"It's Garret."

Rose watched how Garret made an effort to lean down a bit closer each time he spoke to Prentice. He didn't slow his speech as if he were talking to a baby, and his tone carried warmth. More than anything, that convinced her of his character. A man who showed kindness to a gawky little boy had to have a good heart.

"Mr. Garret, wanna know 'bout other mystery gifts?"

"Sure!"

"Mrs. Percopie got a fancy icebox for the diner. Mr. Creek got a great big plow for his farm when the old one broke to smithereens. Hattie's pa got a rifle."

"A Marlin repeating rifle—a fourteen shot," Hugo added. "He's kept that family in meat for the past two winters with the hunting he's done."

"He's quite a hunter," Rose agreed. "Bless his heart, he's been kind enough to give me some delicious roasts."

"Even though I've been here but a short time, Miss Rose," Garret said as he chased a noodle to the edge of his plate and speared it with his fork, "I'd guess you shared every last one of those roasts with someone."

"Roasts were meant to be shared." She smiled. "The Secret Giver sent me a bicycle."

"Do you have any idea who it is?"

Hugo propped his elbows on the table and nodded. "My boss at the bank is wealthy enough. The gifts are all on the expensive side."

"I think it's Mr. Hepplewhite," Prentice said. "He always

finds pennies and nickels behind kids' ears. Maybe he finds money other places, too."

"And what about you, Miss Rose? Do you have a suspicion?"

"Almost everyone in Buttonhole wonders." Rose gave a dainty shrug. "Conjecture is normal enough. My thoughts have taken a different path, though. It occurs to me that more than one individual is capable of showing kindness anonymously."

"She acts all calm now." Hugo chuckled. "You should have seen her the day her bicycle arrived. Our Rose was absolutely giddy."

"I've had hours of enjoyment riding about. Is everyone ready for dessert? I made peach cobbler."

Over a large piece of cobbler, Garret Diamond turned into a sleuth. He and Hugo discussed how the first mystery gift, an organ for the church, arrived the Easter before Rose had moved to Buttonhole. They decided it had to be a husband and wife or a brother and sister. Only a woman would have thought to order a baby's layette with express delivery for Mrs. Andrews when she adopted a foundling. Then, too, they reasoned that only a man would have known the particulars involved in selecting the right plow and would think to include a supply of the proper-sized cartridges with the gift of a quality rifle.

Rose dumped the dishes into the sink to soak while she continued to remedy the scorch in Garret's shirt. Dabbing peroxide on the large mark bleached away much of the discoloration, but she couldn't help inhaling the fragrance of bay rum that drifted up from the fabric. Normally, the homey scent of noodle starch steamed up from her ironing board; Garret's bay rum smelled heady and masculine.

The sheriff dropped by, accepted a chunk of cobbler, and mentioned, "Sneedly's brood is croupy again, and Doc's out on a call. You got anything that'll help out, Rose?"

"Let me see." She excused herself and went into the spare bedroom. Instead of bothering to turn on the gaslight for just the few minutes she'd be there, she'd brought a candle she lit from the stove. The bottom drawer of the five-drawer chest over by the window held her supply of medicaments, and she quickly walked her fingers along the bottles, tins, and jars until she pulled out two items. Holding one container in her hand, the other in the crook of her arm, she managed to grab the candle and return to the gentlemen.

"Sheriff, I do have a couple of things that ought to help a bit." She blew out the candle and set it on the buffet.

"Oh, good." The sheriff pushed away from the table and started to leave. "I hoped you'd scare up a cure. Those kids are barkin' up a storm."

Rose took the bottle from the crook of her arm, jostled it, then held it up to the light. "I'm afraid I'm about out of the Jayne's Expectorant. She looked down at the chunky blue green container in her other hand. "This is a new tin of camphorated salve, though. I'll go over and help make mustard or onion plasters."

"Jayne's?" Garret's brows rose. "Is that stuff any good?"

"Doc recommends it. I think it works fairly well, especially if the children breathe in steam vapor." Rose reached for her cape.

Garret swiped it away and draped it over her shoulders, smoothly enveloping the ample volume of her leg-o'-mutton sleeves. "I have a bucketful of curatives I took out of the store and put in the back until Doc could take a gander at them. A fair number of those bottles strike me as nothing more than false hope. I'm sure I saw a few bottles of Jayne's."

Rose perked up at that bit of news. "With Red Riding Hood on the glass?"

"Oh, is that who it was?" Garret chuckled. "I'll have to take a closer look at the bottle now. We'll drop by the store, and you can check to see if anything else there might help the children."

"Do you mind if I finish your shirt later and return it tomorrow?" She searched for her apron pockets beneath the cape and slipped the bottle and tin into them.

"Not at all. I appreciate your help. It's looking a world better already." He held out his hand. "Why don't you let me carry those?"

"I'd rather ask you to bring the rest of the cobbler, if you don't mind. I doubt Mrs. Sneedly had a chance to cook a decent meal if the children are ill." Rose handed him the still-warm metal pan and swiftly tucked a fresh loaf of bread, a bag of split peas, a hunk of paper-wrapped bacon, and almost a dozen fresh peaches into a flour sack.

"I'll fill your stove while you're gone," Hugo called as she headed toward the door.

"Take your laundry. It's ready to go." She swept out the door. Garret's stride carried him alongside her, and she halted abruptly. "You forgot your suit coat."

"I'll get it tomorrow. Those poor kids are waiting for help."

"More likely, their parents are. The Sneedlys have six children. They've lost half again as many. I've never seen folks suffer so with the hay fever and croup."

"I have a whole bin of onions at the store. Remind me to grab a couple for the poultices."

Rose smiled at him. "Thank you. You know, you could have rubbed a bit of raw onion on the scorch—"

"And made my shirt reek for eternity." They turned the corner, and he led her diagonally across the street so they'd reach his store a few steps faster. "I'd rather lose my shirt to stupidity than to stink."

"Now that Cordelia Orrick has a washing machine, you might hire her to do your laundry."

"Miss Rose, don't you dare try to get me to trade a ring around my collar for a ring through my nose."

seven

"It's nothing short of a modern-day miracle," Cordelia Orrick said for the third time since she'd come into the shop. "A Number Three Western Star washer. A Number Three, mind you! Why, I won't know what to do with all of my spare time now that I won't be using my washboard much."

Zeb Hepplewhite rubbed his nose with the ball of his thumb. "When I got word you'd gotten that newfangled washer, I was hopin' you'd feel thataway. What, with Mrs. Kiersty getting up there in age and battling her quinsy, the laundry's not caught up at my boardinghouse. When it comes to doing the wash, I'm as useless as hip pockets on a hog. Perhaps I could hire you to be the laundress."

Garret smiled to himself and put several new dime novels out onto the shelf. *I'll bet whoever the Secret Giver is, that's what he had planned all along when he ordered that big, new washer.* Whoever the mysterious benefactor was, he seemed to have a knack for selecting practical items—at least most of the time. An icebox for the diner, a plow for a farmer, a hunting rifle for a family man, the washing machine for a mother. . .but a bicycle for Miss Rose seemed like an odd choice.

Why a bicycle? Then again, everyone in Buttonhole seemed to think she was as Mrs. Evert said, "dotty," or as Rose confessed, "dusty in the attic." It stood to reason that the Secret Giver chose something a bit less ordinary for that reason. Besides, hadn't Rose pedaled down Main Street this morning with a basketful of her fresh peaches to share with some townsfolk? He still remembered the supper she'd made. He'd never tasted finer. The woman surely had call to boast about her culinary skills.

He heard the train pull out of the station. About a quarter hour later, the mailbag was brought to the post office—along with a box bearing a label from Sears, Roebuck, and Company for none other than Miss Rose.

Garret argued with himself over the whole matter. Miss Rose was only one person, a maidenly woman of very modest means. How she spent her money was none of his affair. Then again, *where* she spent her money—well, that was his business, or more to the point, it *wasn't* his business. The rest of Buttonhole seemed quite pleased with Diamond Emporium. Folks were voluble in their praise, and sales stayed steady, if not downright brisk compared to what he'd expected from the size of the town and the financial books the previous owner had shown him before he bought the place.

So what if Miss Rose buys things from her catalogue? She comes in here to get her staples and perishables.

It didn't matter. Not really. But it irritated him. Garret took it as a personal challenge. He was going to prove to that woman his store would give her top-notch service, fair prices, and far more convenience than the well-thumbed book she kept on her parlor table. Surely, she could see for herself that he carried superior items.

The bell rang over the door. Garret glanced up and gave a neighborly nod.

"Hello, hello," Lula Mae Evert singsonged. The pink splotches in her cheeks were every bit as bright as the ones painting her daughters' cheekbones. The daughter on the right practically towed her mother along; the taller daughter on Lula Mae's left had to be dragged forward. "Charity and Patience both talked me into letting them have new dresses."

"Mama says you have exquisite yardage." The younger one flashed him a guileless smile.

"How kind of her to say so." He secretly wondered which one was which, but he didn't dare ask. Judging from the way Lula Mae had waxed poetic on Patience's domestic talents, he presumed she was the elder one with the sulky expression.

Lula Mae gushed, "I'm sure my daughters have never seen such lovely trims, either. Why, you have a positively wondrous selection of lace, ribbons, and buttons."

"I'm glad you think so, Mrs. Evert. Take your time, ladies." He gestured toward the area he'd created for the fabrics, patterns, and sewing notions. "I'm sure you'll find something to your liking."

The taller daughter let out a beleaguered sigh. "Sewing is ever so dreary, Mama. Can't you hire a seamstress like Julia's mother?"

Garret couldn't hear what Lula Mae whispered back, but from the set of her jaw, he could tell she wasn't about to put up with her daughter's plan.

A buxom woman who longingly ran her fingers over the Singer treadle sewing machine Garret had on display offered, "I'd be willing to sew for you. I'm planning to turn my parlor into a seamstress shop."

"Thank you, Lacey," Lula Mae said as she cast her daughter a quelling look, "but my daughters are quite adept at sewing."

The older daughter scowled; the shorter daughter continued to smile. She was cute in how she didn't mind that her front teeth overlapped just a bit. Garret didn't doubt that in another year, her mama would instill a self-consciousness about that sweet flaw and drill her until she habitually spoke and laughed behind a gloved hand. For now, though, she reminded him of a little bunny. She scooted into the corner and started to look through the patterns while her sister huffed her dissatisfaction at each bolt of fabric her mother pulled out.

Garret made a mental note about Patience. If the attitude she displayed now was her usual, she wasn't the sort of woman he'd want to share a box supper with, let alone marry. Every pattern required too much work, and each length of fabric elicited a disdainful rejection.

Finally, the younger Miss Evert turned and huffed at her. "Honestly, Patience, if you don't care, I'll pick out something I like. All your dresses get passed down to me, so one of us may as well be happy."

Oh, so I was right. The younger one is Charity. Garret smothered a smile as Patience developed a sudden interest in a length of blue she termed "robin's egg."

"Don't you think this will be ravishing on Patience, Mr. Diamond?" Lula Mae draped a yard around Patience, who glowered at him.

"Pretty as a peacock."

"Same color as one, too," Zeb said from over by the nail barrel.

Patience shoved away the fabric. "I don't care if he's rich, Mama, I'm not—"

"Shh!" Lula Mae fumbled with the bolt and dropped it. Squeezing her daughter's arm to silence her was obviously more important than fine taffeta.

Snorting with glee, Zeb dumped the nails back into the

barrel and folded his arms across his chest. Two ladies standing by the canned goods whispered to one another behind their hands, and Garret hadn't ever been more thankful for the chime on the door. It gave him an excuse to turn away. *Saved by the bell.*

"Isn't it the most gorgeous day?" Rose struggled to fit a pair of baskets into the door. She couldn't seem to look up from them long enough to do more than laugh. Oh, and she laughed so freely. Even with her hands empty, she wouldn't lift one to cover her mouth.

Garret started toward her, but she finally wiggled though. A breeze shut the door behind her, and she tried to take a step, only to have giggles spill out of her.

"Rose, whatever is so entertaining?" Mrs. Kiersty tipped back her head so she could see beneath the brim of her flower-and-ribbon-bedecked straw hat, then looked over the edge of her spectacles.

"I seem to be stuck." Rose shoved one basket into Mrs. Kiersty's hands and the other into Garret's. She twisted to the side, opened the door, and yanked in the portion of her brown paisley skirt that had gotten trapped. Yards of the fabric swept in. What was once probably a pretty gown now qualified as hopelessly bedraggled. It was clean as could be, but the triple row of golden ribbons encircling the hem had puckered, and the hem itself was frayed. Rose didn't seem aware of those flaws. She smoothed the skirt and announced, "There's quite a breeze kicking up."

"Peaches and apricots," Mrs. Kiersty whispered in an oddly rough tone. Garret figured her voice still sounded faint and gravelly from her bout with quinsy. She intently inspected what lay under the basket's blue-and-purple-checkered cloth.

"Fresh from your trees, I presume," Cordelia said as she came over.

"Oh, yes. I just picked them. You'll never imagine what I found while I was picking them!"

Garret felt the basket in his hands move at the same time he heard a small sound. He glanced down and didn't need to imagine. He could see the answer for himself. "Kittens."

"Yes!" Rose lifted a calico bit of fluff and held it high for him to inspect. "Have you ever seen anything so adorable?"

"Rose, Dear, you don't bring wild little animals inside. Certainly, you don't take them into the mercantile." Mrs. Kiersty set aside the basket of fruit and snatched the kitten from her hands by the scruff of the neck. She dumped the mewling baby back into the basket and clucked her tongue. "It's just not done."

Garret agreed—in principle. He just didn't like the way the old biddy plowed in and took charge without regard to Rose's feelings. "He is cute, Rose, but perhaps—"

"Gotta be a shecat." Zeb sauntered over. "Calico cats are always females."

"Everyone's saying the mice are particularly bad this year." Cordelia Orrick picked up a bottle of bluing. Garret presumed she'd also need to buy all of the ingredients for making more laundry soap for her new laundry venture. She set it back down and came over to look at the kittens. He made a mental note to help her gather up all of the necessary chemicals— ammonia, salts of tartar, potash. . .*just as soon as I coax Rose to take her furry little creatures back outside where they belong.*

It made perfect sense for a mercantile to have a mature cat that would prowl the premises at night to keep vermin away. A mouser was a valuable asset; a playful kitten that could tangle yarn, fall into storage bins, or streak out of nowhere and make customers stumble would be a disaster.

Unfortunately, Rose seemed blissfully unaware that Mrs. Kiersty was right and the basket of kittens ought to go. Instead, she petted each kitten with just her forefinger as she told him, "Garret, I heard Tom Cat passed on, and I was sure you'd want one for your back porch to protect your merchandise. You get pick of the litter!"

"You heard about old Tom Cat?"

"Prentice told me. He was terribly upset."

Garret nodded. Just about every afternoon, he'd find Prentice sitting out on the back porch of the mercantile. The boy would have the tattered old tabby on his lap or lazing beside him. The visit never lasted more than ten minutes, but the day old Tom died and Garret saw Prentice's face, he knew the cat meant more to the boy than he'd realized. He'd knelt down to comfort Prentice, but the little guy sobbed a name and ran away. He knew the little boy had gone to Rose for comfort.

"Why don't I let Prentice choose and keep my cat?" *There. Nice solution. Diplomatic. Everyone ought to be satisfied.*

"Cats make Hugo sneeze and itch." Rose smiled at him. "They can't have one, but it's kind of you to offer."

Garret couldn't resist. He reached down and petted the calico. "He could keep one at your house."

Rose continued to smile. "I kept the runt."

"Isn't that just like you?" Patience Evert simpered.

Garret looked at the young woman and could see by her patently insincere smile that she'd not meant it in a complimentary way, but her mother gushed, "It is. Rose has a soft spot in her heart for anything or anyone that's. . .different."

"Why, thank you, Lula Mae." Rose smiled at her.

"Mama, isn't the tabby cute?" Charity wiggled through the knot of people and scooped one of the pale orange ones out of the basket. She lifted it and giggled as he started to climb up her sleeve.

"You're ruining your dress," Patience snapped.

"Don't let it near your collar." Lula Mae flapped her hands fretfully. "His claws will shred the lace."

"And that's Belgian lace," Mrs. Kiersty whispered as she adjusted her spectacles and repinned her hat farther back on her head. She leaned in so she could see it better. "I remember that piece from when you made it for Patience. Pretty as a snowflake."

"And it was stylish back then," Patience tacked on.

Rose reached over and covered Charity's hand with her own so they both stroked the kitten together. "Style may be fleeting, but beauty and grace are eternal."

"That's what I taught my daughters, too." Mrs. Kiersty bobbed her head so emphatically, Garret marveled her hat didn't flip off and roll away. Surely that one hatpin wasn't designed to withstand such a challenge. She glared pointedly at the basket, which held only one kitten now since Cordelia cupped the other tabby to herself and Zeb was tickling it with its own white-tipped tail. "But I taught them that animals belong outside."

Garret fished out the calico Rose originally held out to him and set aside the empty basket. "These are fine little beasts." *I don't want a cat.*

"Aren't they?" Rose beamed at him.

"Mama, could I keep this one?" Charity gave her mother a pleading look. "I'll give up having a new dress."

Whoops. This little basket of trouble is cutting into my business.

I need to get it out of here.

"You don't need a cat." Her mother took the kitten from her. "You need a dress."

Whew.

The tabby rubbed his head back and forth against Lula Mae. The woman melted faster than a chip of ice in the sun. "Aww. He is a precious little thing."

"Mr. Diamond, you were to choose first." Cordelia Orrick looked like she'd burst into tears if he took the tabby she held.

"I don't need a cat. Why don't you take that one? He certainly looks at home in your arms."

Cordelia perked up. "Oh, and since Rose found him in a peach tree and he's this color, I'll name him Mr. Peaches!"

"And ours can be called Apricot—Cottie for short," Charity decided.

"Two down, one to go." Zeb looked pointedly at the one in Garret's hands.

"I just said I didn't want a cat. Why don't you take him, Zeb?"

Zeb held his hands out, palms upward. "Nuh-unh."

Garret raised his brows. "How about you, Mrs. Kiersty? Wouldn't you enjoy this little ball of fur when you're out in that handsome garden you've planted?"

For a moment, her face lit up.

Hurrah! Did it. That was easy enough.

"I said no, and she lives and works at my boardinghouse." Zeb's words cut short Garret's premature self-congratulations.

"He'd dig up my garden anyway," Mrs. Kiersty said with a sigh. "I used fish in the mulch." Zeb took her arm and pulled her toward the door. They scurried out as if Garret would chase her down and slip the cat under her hat if she didn't get away fast enough. The other two ladies who had been twittering behind their hands and the one by the sewing machine followed in their tracks.

The little calico kitten started to purr loudly. The vibrations beneath Garret's fingertips enticed him to continue stroking her.

"I need to check in on Mrs. Kendricks, Garret. Remember when her son, Trevor, stopped in to buy embroidery floss for her? She's still unwell. Even if you don't want to give that kitten a home, could you keep her for an hour or so?"

He cleared his throat and nodded.

"Thank you." Rose picked up the fruit basket, and Cordelia grabbed hold of her arm.

"I'll walk with you. You can stop in for a moment to see my new washer. It's a Number Three Western Star!"

They left, and Lula Mae clasped the tabby to her bodice. "Since Patience can't decide on material, we'll just take this baby home and settle him in."

The door closed, and Garret looked around the store. Empty. Completely empty. He'd had seven—no, eight—customers in here just moments ago. He lifted the calico kitten so they were nose to nose. It let out a tiny meow and continued to purr loudly.

"Stop sounding so content. Everyone just left, and not a one of them bought a single thing."

eight

"Garret, I'm afraid I owe you an apology," Rose said as she hurried up to the mercantile.

Garret stopped sweeping the boardwalk and turned to face her. His brows knit. "I beg your pardon?"

Rose laughed. "You have that backward. I was begging your pardon. I got busy with Mrs. Kendricks and lost track of the time. You've been stuck playing nanny for a kitten you don't want."

He folded both hands on the end of the broom and extended his arms fully. The sleeve fabric pulled until the green-and-black-striped garters no longer left even the slightest ripple in the length. Other than the barber, who always looked awkward and silly as he swept, Rose couldn't think of any other man she'd seen with a broom in his hands. Garret managed to make the broom look every bit as masculine a tool as a rifle or ax.

Rose batted away a ribbon from her hat that fluttered against her cheek. "I came to collect the kitten and hope you'll accept an invitation to supper as restitution."

"That depends."

"On what?"

"Yes, on what—what we're having for supper. And if you're making one of your scrumptious cobblers for dessert. Minding kittens isn't without its dangers."

"Oh, no!" Terrible images of what havoc the kitten must

68

have wreaked in the store flashed before her eyes. "What did the kitty do?"

"Nothing too terrible. Just kept me on my toes. She seems to like tight places."

"Tight places?" Rose echoed back the words and had a sick feeling inside.

Garret shrugged and took a few last swipes with the broom. "She tried to hide behind the shovels and such. While I picked them up, she crept behind the brooms."

Rose groaned. She could picture it all vividly—shovels, hoes, and rakes tumbling down. "I'm ever so sorry, Garret."

"Her adventures tired her out. She took a nice nap."

Rose let out a small sigh of relief.

"On the blankets. Scared Mrs. Blanchard out of a year's growth, I'm afraid."

Dread laced her words. "Where is she now?"

"Mrs. Blanchard or the kitten?"

"Both." That one word stuck in her throat and came out like she was being strangled.

Garret opened the door and motioned her inside. She'd just begun to cross the threshold when he said, "Mrs. Blanchard is at home with a new bottle of smelling salts."

"Smelling salts?"

"I'll have to order more. They were quite effective." He set the broom in the corner and wiped his hands on a damp dishcloth he had hanging from a wooden ring by the counter.

Rose's nose twitched. The mercantile used to smell mostly of dust. At the grand opening, she'd noticed a wonderful mingling of lemon and beeswax, pickles, new leather, and fresh apples and oranges. This morning, it had carried that same delicious mix of aromas. Now, all she could smell was dill.

Garret leaned his hips against the counter and rested his hands on either side of him. He looked utterly relaxed as he casually stated, "Pickle is upstairs in my bedroom."

"Pickle." Rose's head swivelled to the side. The three-gallon glass jar that usually rested on the far side of the counter was gone. The dill smell permeating the mercantile suddenly made sense. She covered her face with both hands and burst out laughing.

Ten minutes later, Garret handed her a dipper of water. She'd laughed herself right into a fit of hiccups. "I'm sorry. *Hic.* Truly I am, Garret. You know I'll—*hic*—gladly reimburse you for the pick—*hic*—kle jar and the smelling s—*hic*—salts. I'll stay and scrub your—*hic*—counter with soda. That ought to take a—*hic*—way some of the dill."

"Stop apologizing and tell me: If we bathe the kitten in soda, will it take the smell off of her?"

Rose choked on the water and barely kept from spewing it everywhere. "She didn't just—*hic*—knock over the jar?"

"I'm afraid not. She must've thought the pickle was a fish. When the jar fell, the brine washed right over the kitty. The only thing I could think of was that tomato juice is supposed to take care of skunk odor. I'd resigned myself to smashing a few dozen tomatoes in one of the galvanized tubs and dunking Pickle in it."

"Pickle and catsup?" Rose hiccuped and started laughing anew.

Garret chuckled. "I wasn't brave enough to do it on my own. I can just see that little scamp wiggling away and leaving a red streak all over the store."

Rose drew in a deep breath and spoke as rapidly as she could in hopes that she'd manage to say everything before she hiccupped again. "I'll take her home and get her cleaned up. After you—*hic*—close the store, come over for supper. I'll give you a choice: roast—*hic*—chicken or panfried pork chops."

He motioned her to take another sip of water. "What about my apple cobbler?"

The water seemed to banish her affliction. She handed back the dipper. "I'll bake two cobblers, and you can bring the second one back to have all to yourself. It's the least I can do after what the kitten did."

Garret didn't leave to fetch the cat. He set aside the dipper, folded his arms across his chest, and rocked from heel to toe and back again. "You can't bathe the cat without me. I get to watch."

Rose bent to pick up the basket in which she'd brought the cat. As she straightened, she caught the ornery twinkle in Garret's eyes.

"So the old saying is true," he mused aloud. The corner of his mouth tugged into a rakish smile.

"What saying?"

He looked pointedly at the basket, then scanned the mercantile as he drawled, "Criminals return to the scene of the crime."

"How am I to know that you didn't teach that poor, innocent kitty all of those bad habits? She never knocked things over, scared the wits out of a woman, or broke anything at my house."

"It's a woman thing. I'm sure of it. She was trying to rearrange my store, was being catty about Mrs. Blanchard's bilious-colored dress, and gave in to a temper fit. I'll bet you found the kittens because she was causing a ruckus and threw peaches at you."

"Garret Diamond, you missed your calling in life." She picked up one of the dime novels and waved it like a fan in front of herself. "With the tales you make up, you should have become an author."

❧

"Rose Masterson, you missed your calling in life," Garret said half an hour later as they stood on opposite sides of a table she'd set up. "This arrangement you have here could turn into quite an enterprise."

An old maple table sat in the middle of her yard. Two buckets and a pair of wash tubs sat on it—all full of warm water. In the middle of the table were a scrub brush and a box of baking soda, and two more full buckets waited on the grass under the table. A stack of towels sat on a chair behind her. He nodded approvingly. "Everything necessary to bathe a cat."

"Don't go making any grandiose proclamations yet. The second I get that cat wet, we're going to be wet. I gave the runt a bath this morning, which is why I have twice as much water and three towels."

Garret unbuttoned his sleeves and rolled them up. For good measure, he used the garters to hike his sleeves up past the muscles of his forearms. "I'm not about to let a cat get the better of me."

Five minutes later, Garret shot Rose a quick look, then grabbed Pickle by the scruff of the neck and struggled to wiggle her so she'd let go of the edge of the tub. He'd barely managed to dunk her the first time, and she'd shot out of the tub with a hair-raising yowl. Rose managed to dump half of the box of soda into the water, and she tried to use the scrub brush to help work more into the kitten's fur.

"Watcha doin'?" Prentice asked from the other side of the sagging fence.

"Washing a kitty." Rose sucked in a quick breath as Pickle scratched her wrist. "Oh, dear."

In a matter of minutes, several of Buttonhole's children and a few of the adults were witnesses to the remainder of the kitten's bath. Afterward, as Prentice sat and held a towel-wrapped Pickle, Rose served peach cobbler to everyone. Garret sighed and told her to cut into the second pan—his pan. Rose giggled. "I imagine since you've never seen my backyard, you're hoping the peach tree is large."

"Guilty as charged, Miss Rose."

"It's rather small." She paused strategically. "But the other two peach trees toward the back of the yard are huge."

"I'll make it a point to come peach picking, Miss Rose." He took up a few plates and helped her serve the rest of that second cobbler, and Rose licked the last of the sweet peachy syrup from her silver server. Having a scamp like Garret over to pick peaches suited her just fine.

"Know what?" Prentice announced in a loud voice to everyone while conscientiously keeping hold of the cat. "Mr. Diamond is Miss Rose's beau. She called him 'dear.'"

❦

"Balderdash." Garret turned to her, then immediately added, "I mean you no disrespect, Miss Rose."

She laughed. "I took none. Prentice, I said, 'Oh, dear,' just as your mama used to say, 'Oh, my,' or Mrs. Busby says, 'Mercy me.'"

"I've never heard such piffle. Rose isn't the marrying type at all," Lula Mae singsonged. "Rose, you simply must give me your recipe for this cobbler. It melts in my mouth."

"I'll write it down for you and bring you peaches tomorrow."

Garret frowned at Rose. "You oughtn't be picking peaches—not with those scratches."

"I have peroxide."

"Yes," Hugo chuckled. "Remember? She used it on your scorched shirt."

Cordelia frowned. "I can bandage those scratches while I'm here. Where do you keep your peroxide?"

"The bottom drawer in the spare bedroom."

"You stay out here and mind your daughters. I'll fetch it," Mrs. Blanchard said. Garret suspected her motive was less to help than it was to get away from the cat. Chances were good the only reason Mrs. Blanchard had stopped by in the first place was because this impromptu gathering featured a sweet and a chance to chat. For being as skinny as she was, the woman had a terrible sweet tooth. She stopped into the store each day to get a full penny's worth of candy, and Rose's cobbler rated as far more desirable.

Neighbors drifted off, and Mrs. Blanchard reappeared with the peroxide, a dishcloth, and some salve. She clucked her tongue as she set them down on the water-splashed table beside the tubs and buckets Garret had emptied and stacked. "Silly woman. She's playing with kittens when there's dust at least half an inch thick in her spare room and parlor." She spiraled her finger in the air right beside her temple and whispered, "I tell you, she's touched."

Garret lifted the dishcloth Mrs. Blanchard had brought out and studied it. Made from an old white flour sack, it still bore the faintest outline of Minnesota Pink Label. On the opposite side and end, Rose had embroidered, "Sunday" and a cheery-looking sunshine in the corner. He continued to look at that silly decoration and said softly, "I, for one, am glad she used her time to bake those cobblers instead of dusting. Aren't you, Mrs. Blanchard?"

"There's no law that says she couldn't do both." The woman stuck her nose in the air and stomped off.

Hugo steered Prentice past the table and across the street. They were the last to go. Rose stood by the porch holding Pickles while the runt she'd mentioned slept on the windowsill behind her. Garret called over, "Rosie, put down the cat, and let's take care of your scratches."

Angry weals lined the full length of all the thin, long scratches. Garret frowned as he inspected her wrists. "I know you already washed these, but I think you'd best suds them again. Cat scratches are known for causing infections and fevers."

"Oh, a splash of peroxide will do me just fine."

Garret wouldn't let her pull her hands from his. "Soap first. I'll apply peroxide, then some salve. What about bandaging them for the night?"

"Stuff and nonsense!"

He gave her a stern look. "If this were anyone else, you'd insist on that treatment."

Rose let out an irked sound, but she didn't deny the truth. "Would it satisfy you if I promised to apply salve and to wear gloves tonight?"

"It'll spoil your gloves—make them greasy." As he spoke, he dipped her hands into a fresh pail of water and gently washed the scratches. Such wonderful hands she had. Her nails were short, her fingers slim and long. Instead of being milky white, her hands and wrists carried the slightest bit of coloring—no doubt from the hours she spent gardening and picking fruit. The backs of her hands were soft as could be, but the palms bore small calluses that tattled on how she wasn't afraid of pitching in and doing work. They reminded him of his great-aunts, Brigit and Emily. They'd spent a lifetime of doing good deeds, and he'd considered their hands beautiful.

Rose slipped her hands from his and cupped them, palms upward. She pursed her lips and blew, sending bubbles floating into the wind. Her laughter floated along with them as she dunked her fingers to rinse off the remainder of the soap. As she dried her palms on the Sunday dishcloth, she asked, "Did I tell you that 'Pickle' is a marvelous name for the kitten? You'll have to help me think of a name for the runt."

Garret carefully applied the peroxide, watched it bubble, then applied the ointment. "I see his coloring is like the other two."

"Yes, there was only one calico. The runt is a girl, though. Any ideas for her name?"

He slowly stroked the salve along the next scratch. Most of the time, women wore gloves. This contact with Rose seemed so warm, so personal. He was in no mood to rush through it. "Mr. Peaches, Apricot, and Pickles. The others are named for food. I'm trying to think of something that's orangey-tan. Crackers? Caramel? Cobbler?"

Rose shook her head. "Cobbler would be too confusing. I like Caramel. That's cute." Her nose wrinkled.

"Did I hurt you?" He paused and continued to gently hold her hand.

"Oh, no. Not at all. I was just thinking that Pickle and Caramel make for an odd couple of names." To his acute disappointment, she pulled away and left him feeling oddly incomplete as a result.

"If anything. . ." She paused to laugh again. "When I call them, it's probably going to give everyone fodder to think I'm slipping further into my nonsensical morass."

"Rose, I'm about convinced your attic isn't dusty—it's drafty as can be if you think I'm letting you keep my cat." He dumped out the bucket, scooped up Pickle, and walked off. He was halfway back to the store before he realized something. Pickle didn't smell of dill brine any longer. The faint but unmistakable fragrance of tea rose wafted from her fur.

He threw back his head and laughed. Rose had anointed his cat with her perfume!

nine

"Let's try it again." Rose cupped her hands around the harmonica and watched as Prentice bobbed his head and drew in a deep breath. He lifted his own nickel-plated Hohner harmonica, and they started to play a duet.

"I think Susannah would say, 'Oh!' all right if she heard us play that," Prentice moaned after they finished. "Miss Rose, we sound terr'ble."

"I've heard better," she admitted. "I know we wanted to keep this a secret, but perhaps it's time for us to seek out help. Who do we know who plays a harmonica?"

Prentice stuck out his tongue through the empty spot where his teeth once were and played with the gap. "I dunno."

"Hello."

Rose jumped a bit and swivelled around. "Garret!" She motioned him over enthusiastically. "What a wonderful surprise. What brings you here?"

He opened the gate and sauntered into her backyard with long, lazy strides that still managed to close the distance between them quite quickly. "Cordelia Orrick is minding the store. I came to pick peaches."

Prentice elbowed her and whispered loudly, "Ask him!"

"Ask me what?"

Rose lifted her harmonica. "Can you make this silly thing work?"

"I've been known to puff a tune or two." Garret accepted it

and polished the nickel on his sleeve. He took a seat on the step next to Rose. "The first trick is, you have to shine it up and make sure it's warm. A cold one makes your mouth stick so the mouth organ won't slide easily."

"Wow. He's gonna be great!" Prentice hopped up, raced over, and plopped back down on Garret's other side.

There wasn't enough room, so Garret scooted closer. Rose gathered her skirts and started to inch away, but he curled his arm around her shoulders and halted her movement. "You needn't run away, Miss Rose. I promise not to deafen you with too many sour notes."

She smiled. "I'm just scooting over a tad."

"Better not. You'll fall in that—what is that thing?" He leaned forward and squinted.

"A strawberry barrel. By cutting holes all over in the barrel, I can harvest a fine crop of berries in a small space."

Garret's arm tightened, and he yanked her closer. Rose muffled a surprised squeal. "That settles it! I hold a definite liking for both you and strawberries, so I refuse to let you fall."

Rose couldn't remember the last time someone had hugged her. The feeling of being sheltered washed over her. Garret's easygoing nature and scampish smile made her settle in close beside him with a contented sigh. Life couldn't be richer or sweeter than to have good friends, a sunny day, and be surrounded by the blessing of God's bounty.

Rose watched as Garret cradled the harmonica like she would hold a tiny chick. An odd thought streamed through her mind. *I like the way he moves—his confident, steady gait, the effortless manner in which he hefts heavy things, the supple gestures he uses, and now—the way he wraps those long-fingered, strong hands around the little instrument.*

"Here's how you do it." He patiently showed Prentice how to hold the harmonica, tricks on how to sense and hear the right notes, and how to play as he both inhaled and exhaled. Soon, Prentice was playing recognizable snippets from songs.

"You taught him more in fifteen minutes than I have in three weeks," Rose praised.

"You practice more, little man. Rose is going to hold a basket for me while I pick fruit." Garret held up a finger to silence her before she could protest. "You are not going to pick anything until those scratches are completely healed."

"They're already much better." She held them up and wiggled her fingers.

"Miss Rose," Garret said in a low tone as his brows knit, "you'd best be thankful your yard doesn't have a hickory tree in it."

"Hickory?" She glanced around, then gave him a baffled look. "Why?"

"Where I come from, folks got a whuppin' with a hickory switch for stretching the truth beyond all recognition."

Rose tilted her nose in the air. "I'm not telling a falsehood. They've not festered as cat scratches can, and I kept salve on them all night."

"You ought to soak them."

"I did." When he gave her a stern look, she sheepishly added, "In a manner of speaking. They were in warm water whilst I washed the dishes."

"You've misbehaved enough for the day, if not for the week." Garret handed her an empty basket. "You just stand there. I'll fill it." He reached up and plucked two peaches from a branch and placed them in the basket.

"This is ridiculous. I want to be useful."

"You can be useful by deciding where all of these. . ." He picked two more and held them up before tucking them in the basket with the others. "Are going to end up."

"They're all coming ripe at the same time. I'll can as much as possible." She tipped her head back and looked up at the heavily laden branches. "I have enough to feed an army."

"I have empty crates at the emporium." His movements were so fluid, it didn't seem as if he was working at all, yet the basket she held was filling up fast. He paused a moment and looked at her. "We could send peaches to the orphanage in Roanoke. Don't you think those children would enjoy them?"

"What a wonderful idea! The train comes through tomorrow morning. We could do that, couldn't we?"

"I have a feeling we could do just about anything we put our minds to."

"As long as the Lord blessed the task," she tacked on.

"Look at all of this. It would be a sin to waste it. After you decide how much you want to keep for your own use, I'd be happy to carry some to the boardinghouse." He took the full basket from her, set it on the steps next to Prentice, who continued to puff into his harmonica with more zeal than talent, then came back with another basket.

Rose had already picked three peaches. She lay them in the basket, and Garret groused at her, "You need to learn to follow directions, Woman. No more picking. You just hold this."

"You're downright bossy, Garret Diamond."

"If my skin were as thin as the skin on these peaches, I'd be mortally wounded by your harsh words."

"Doc Rexfeld is talented." She laughed. "I'm sure he could pull you through."

"He was just in the store yesterday. Struck me as a competent, likeable fellow." He rapidly filled that basket. "Hey, speaking of the emporium, I wouldn't mind putting some of your fruit out. You could make a bit of money on all of these extra peaches and apricots, you know."

"Oh, I couldn't! I'd much rather give them away." She lifted the basket higher. As it filled, it grew increasingly heavy.

Garret hitched his right shoulder. "If that's what you want. I'd be willing to give you some jars or sugar if you want to can or preserve more. Knowing you, you'll be giving most of it away."

His generosity and enthusiasm for giving to others touched her deeply. "I really have enough jars. Could I talk you into giving the jars to Cordelia? Her girls love peaches, but she's sensitive about taking charity. Perhaps if you worked it out as part of her pay. . ."

"I still have some of those I emptied when I took over the emporium. I'll just stick them in a wagon and have Prentice wheel them over to her house. If you take the peaches over tomorrow, she's bound to—"

Prentice came over. "Listen to this!" He played "Three Blind Mice" with just enough accuracy to allow them to guess the tune.

Garret gently rubbed a freshly picked peach on his sleeve and handed it to the little boy. "That deserves a prize. Here you are." As they finished filling the bucket, he brushed a leaf off Rose's shoulder and puffed out her sleeve.

Rose laughed. "I'm a wreck, and you did all the work."

"All the work? We're not stopping already. I haven't even gotten to climb a tree yet."

She looked from the tree to him, then back at the branches.

"I don't even let Prentice climb the peach, apricot, or plum trees. The limbs aren't strong enough to bear weight."

"Killjoy."

She couldn't believe her ears. "Did you just call me a name?"

He grabbed the bucket from her and leaned close enough that the sparkle in his eyes warned her he might say something outrageous. "Well, I guess I'll take solace in the fact that Prentice's harmonica playing didn't harm your hearing." He added, raising his voice, "Even if you are a spoilsport."

"Oh. Are they spoiled, Miss Rose?" Prentice pouted. "You were going to make jam."

Garret took that as an invitation to harvest several more bushels. They picked peaches and apricots aplenty. He carried a few of the baskets into the kitchen and set them on the table.

Rose scampered alongside and tried to reach the table first, but she didn't quite manage. The Sears catalogue lay open to the pages featuring sewing machines, and Garret leaned forward to study the selection. "What are you getting?"

Rose slammed the book shut and stammered, "The, uh, moquette rug," she barely choked out.

"I see." He folded his arms across his chest and drummed his fingers on the opposite upper arms. "I have moquette rugs. Just got in a nice selection. What color were you thinking of?"

"Medium. It's floral." Rose reached up and loosened the suddenly-too-tight collar band on her shirt. "I just want a yard of it to put by the sink."

"Medium isn't much of a color. That's one of the drawbacks of dealing with catalogue purchases. You're buying things sight unseen. You can choose exactly the hue that suits your fancy at my mercantile."

"I like being surprised."

"I see. Well, I need to be getting back to the store."

He picked up the envelope next to the catalogue and offered, "Would you like me to post this since I'm going back to the store?"

"I'd appreciate it." *Though I'd have been far happier if you'd never seen it.* She smiled. "Thank you, Garret."

Without another word, he walked out of her house.

Rose sank onto a chair and crumpled her apron and skirt in her fists. *Oh, no. Oh, I never wanted this to happen.*

Prentice came in. The door banged behind him. "Miss Rose, can I take my ha'mon'ca home now? It's not a secret anymore."

"Huh? Oh. Yes." She blinked at him and forced a smile. "Sure, Honey. Go right on ahead. I want you to enjoy it."

"You gonna give away all this stuff, or are you baking with it?" Prentice wore a toothless smile as he tucked the harmonica in his shirt pocket. He helped himself to an apricot, twisted it in half, and ate the half without the pit. Juice slid down the edge of his hand.

"There's gracious plenty. I'll probably share some, can some for the winter, and do a bit of baking. How does that sound?"

"Could you dry some of these 'cots again like you did last year? Daddy and me really liked them."

"Sure. Why don't you help me when you come home from school tomorrow?"

" 'Kay." He licked the juice, then popped the other half of the apricot into his mouth and went to the dustbin, where he proceeded to spit out the pit. The sound it made when it hit the metal never ceased to make him smile.

Rose grinned along with him. She'd taught him that perfectly horrid trick not long after Mary Ellen died. Prentice had been crying for days and had no appetite, so in an attempt to get him to calm down and try to eat, Rose demonstrated that vile stunt. He'd been entranced. She counted it a true miracle that the boy didn't end up with a miserable bellyache that night, because he'd eaten a full dozen apricots.

Rose looked at the bushels and didn't feel her usual sense of contentment. Instead of representing God's providence and a way to bless others, those bushels served as a reminder that Garret had picked each piece of fruit and shared a perfectly enjoyable afternoon with her. Then, that catalogue had spoiled it all.

Garret had made marvelous changes at the mercantile and took the time to assure her he'd gladly order or carry any item she desired. He'd even looked at her catalogue one afternoon and proven that with the shipping costs added on, the items she'd mail-ordered weren't any better a bargain than what he kept conveniently on hand right there in Buttonhole.

But she'd ordered that dumb rug from her catalogue, and he'd found out. The rug was like almost everything else she ordered—just an excuse to send an envelope to Sears. Everyone in Buttonhole thought she was a woman of very modest means, and the poor condition of the mercantile in the past few years had given her ample reason to choose to do business by mail order.

But now—Garret is sharp as can be, and I was careless. How could I have left the catalogue open like that? To the sewing machines, of all things! I didn't lie. I really did order a yard of that stupid carpeting—but the envelope is heavy and has two stamps on it, and the carpet will only be a dollar. Why didn't

I think of something else? I hope he's too busy to notice the enve-
lope is too thick for just one dollar, or he's likely to figure out that
I'm the Secret Giver.

ten

"Good day," Garret said, returning Mr. Sowell's greeting. At least part of that statement was true. He'd felt quite free, taking his very first afternoon off since he'd come to town. The young Widow Orrick proved to be quite able to help out at the store, so he'd gone off to spend his time with Rose.

They'd had a wonderful time in the yard, picking fruit. Prentice scared away the birds with his awful harmonica playing, but Rose's laughter more than made up for the shrill notes. The envelope rested in his coat pocket, the slight weight of it taunting him. Everything was fine until he saw that atrocious catalogue—but Garret refused to let that darken his mood.

He'd assessed Rose Masterson from the start and known she'd be a tough customer. He'd never met a more independent woman—she knew what she wanted, and nothing else would satisfy her. He could normally entice a customer to try something new or buy a little something different. It would really test his salesmanship to get the hardest customer to switch her allegiance from Sears to his emporium, and that person was Rose.

Nonetheless, he liked the challenge.

He nodded emphatically as he told himself that with time and patience, he was going to prove his mercantile worthy of all of her patronage.

"Well, as I live and breathe! It's you, Mr. Diamond—out for a constitutional in the middle of a workday?"

Garret turned toward Mrs. Patterson's voice. She held a watering can, and the potted plants along her porch rail dripped down the railing, leaving a muddy streak. Finicky as Mrs. Patterson was, she'd undoubtedly wash the streak away. "Hello, Mrs. Patterson! Are you enjoying that new rocking chair?"

"Absolutely." She beamed and beckoned. "Come see how lovely it looks in our parlor." As he walked up to the porch, he quelled a smile. She'd leaned over the railing and used the last little bit of water to rinse off the unsightly streak so her house would be picture-perfect.

After he agreed the rocker she'd purchased looked far better in her home than in his store, Garret got a sinking feeling as Mrs. Patterson gave him a calculated smile. "It's quite hot today. You must join Missy and me on the veranda for a glass of sweet tea."

He drank enough sweet tea to float the Spanish Armada. While Mrs. Patterson filled his glass yet again, Missy dutifully mouthed another oh-so-appropriate platitude about the weather. "Don't you simply adore this breeze?"

He nodded. "Very refreshing."

"The blossoms are setting nicely." She smoothed her skirts needlessly. "Mama says we'll have a bumper crop of tomatoes. Daddy says the *Farmer's Almanac* predicted that, too."

"I suppose you'll be busy canning them."

"Oh, Missy loves working in the kitchen, don't you, Dear?" Mrs. Patterson prompted.

Missy nodded obediently and blotted the corner of her mouth with a spotless linen napkin.

She is just what I should be looking for. Pretty. Gentle and poised, too. But Garret couldn't help comparing her polished ways to Rose's engaging exuberance. He hoped he wasn't too abrupt when he took his leave.

He saw Mrs. Sneedly on the street and asked about the children. "Hale as can be now, thanks to Rose. Thanks be to God, too!"

"I'm glad to hear they've improved."

"So am I." Mrs. Sneedly bobbed her head. "And since they're so much better, Anna is able to fiddle around in the kitchen again. Why, she's famous hereabouts for her carrot cake."

"Is that so?"

"Absolutely. You mustn't think I'm exaggerating just because she's my daughter. Why, the parson's wife herself suggested that Anna enter her carrot cake in the county fair."

"That's quite a compliment."

"You'll have to come by and sample it for yourself."

Garret managed to bring the conversation to a close and wandered off. Any man would love a woman who could cook like Anna, and she was tame and biddable as could be. Her apron was always spotless, and he'd never seen her go out without a hat. She didn't have Rose's fire and zest for the simple things like using a blade of grass for a whistle. Life would be very predictable with Anna.

I always thought I wanted an easygoing woman who'd be like her—she'd be proper and excellent at keeping the store neat as a pin. What's the matter with me that there are a half-dozen suitable women in town, and the only one who appeals to me is stubborn, wild little Rose?

He thought about going back to the store, but as he drew closer, he could see Cordelia through the window. Cordelia had a pair of stockings draped over her shoulder and was holding up one of the expensive, lace-edged, Madame Mystique corset covers for a customer's approval.

That in itself was enough to make him hesitate about entering, but then he saw Lula Mae in there with Mrs. Blanchard. Not a day went by that those two women didn't come into his store on some flimsy pretext or another. Lula Mae sang her daughter Patience's praises, and Mrs. Blanchard made her daughter Constance sound like a paragon of every virtue known to man.

The two mothers had practically used him as a tug-o'-war rope after church last week, each asserting he ought to come to *her* home for Sunday supper. Bless her heart, Rose had breezed over and tucked her hand in the crook of his arm. "Hugo and Prentice look like they're wilting with hunger, and I made that peach cobbler you all like so much. Are we ready to go now?"

"I sure am, Miss Rose."

If he went in the mercantile now, those two mamas would start in on their matrimonial machinations again, and he refused to put himself in the middle of such nonsense. He'd like to choose his own wife, thank you very much. Quite frankly, at this moment, he'd had enough. He didn't think he could endure one more conversation. He had some thinking to do. He cut to the back alley and headed down Elm Street to escape that encounter.

Garret tried to think of a place he'd like to go. If he went to the diner, Mrs. Percopie would be sure to have her daughter serve him, then she'd give Hattie a break so she could sit a spell.

Absently, Garret reached up and smoothed his hair. He could use a haircut, and the barbershop had to be safe. It was the town's male bastion—a place where he could escape mothers and the countless tales of their daughters' accomplishments. It would feel good to get a trim and a shave—to relax and not have to listen to the fluttering of Cupid's wings.

Garret walked in to an empty shop. Mr. Busby gestured toward the chair. "Have a seat."

Garret eased onto the red leather seat, leaned back, and closed his eyes. Peace. Safety. He let out a sigh of unmitigated relief.

Mr. Busby pulled the comb through Garret's hair. "Same cut as the first time you came in?"

"Yep."

Mr. Busby whistled a few notes through his teeth. Garret couldn't help thinking he sounded a lot like Prentice on the harmonica. *Snip. Snip. Comb. Snip.*

"So how are you liking Buttonhole?"

"Great town. Glad I came."

The barber grunted his agreement. *Snip. Snip.* "Great place to settle down."

"I can see that."

"Next thing you know, you'll be wanting to marry up." Mr. Busby shifted and started snipping at a different place. "Got a handful of pretty gals, but none better than my niece. I'm sure you've met her—Missy. Missy Patterson."

"I saw her at church." Garret didn't want to say much. He could end up bald or butchered. He kept silent as Busby dropped endless, anvil-like "hints" that Missy would make a fine wife.

"So ready for a shave, too?" Busby already had the razor in hand and had smacked it across the strop.

Garret pulled off the towel and shook his head. "Not

today. Thanks." He paid for the haircut and walked out as fast as decorum permitted.

Garret walked until he hit the edge of town. He didn't want to talk to anyone now. His thoughts shifted to Rose Masterson, and suddenly there she was—a streak of dust on her cheek, a dirty cloth hanging out of her pocket, and Dutch-clean windows sparkling behind her as she pushed Old Hannah's wheeled invalid chair into a shady spot.

He ought to keep walking, but he couldn't force himself to. Garret couldn't take his eyes off of Rose. Why would a woman with her warm, sensitive spirit purposefully conduct her business with a mail-order company located outside her own community instead of with someone she'd invited to dine at her very own table? Things didn't add up.

Why was the catalogue open to sewing machines if she was buying carpeting? Rose didn't sew much, or her clothes would be newer or in better condition. Lacey Norse positively coveted the sewing machine at the mercantile; Rose hadn't paid more than fleeting attention to it. She'd just swish by it and head to Mr. Deeter's post office window and mail a letter.

Rose had no family. She'd once mentioned in conversation that she rarely corresponded with her old friends—they'd married and grown busy with children. Yet she mailed off something each week or so. The envelope he'd promised to mail for her was heavy—too heavy to contain a single dollar. Garret stared at her as realization dawned.

Within in minutes, Rose's arms were full of lavender and pink sweet peas, and she set them on the frail old woman's lap. Garret watched as Rose picked up a tendril of the pink flowers and pinned them around the lady's sparse little bun.

"Hannah, you look like an angel with a halo!"

Garret cleared his throat. Both women looked up at him. He shook his head. "Ma'am, I beg to differ. You look like a queen." He focused his attention on Rose. She'd frozen in place, her fingers still hovering over Old Hannah's hair. She met his gaze, stepped away from the old woman, and wiped her hands on the sides of her dress.

"You need to stop by the mercantile on your way home, Rose."

ঝ

Rose wished that bell over the mercantile door didn't clang so loudly. The town didn't have a bell for the church, but this one was noisy enough that they ought to wrestle it from Garret Diamond and stick it in the steeple! Her gaze darted about the emporium. No one was there. Mr. Deeter had already closed the post office.

What am I doing here? I'm a modern woman. I don't need a man to dictate my actions. I tend to my own matters. I have the right to order goods from anywhere I want, anytime I want. What business does Garret have, ordering me to make an appearance? I can't believe I actually listened to him and came in here! I don't owe him an explanation for what I buy from Sears and Roebuck.

She made an impatient noise at her foolishness for obeying such a high-handed order and wheeled about to march out the door.

"You're not running away, are you?"

She closed her eyes and muffled a moan.

Garret climbed down from the ladder and dusted his hands as she slowly turned back around.

Rose didn't want to look him in the eye after she'd complied with his command, so she glanced up and saw the new banner he'd hung that advertised Calder's Saponaceous Dentine. She said the first thing that came to mind. "Are you trying to sell that stuff or give small children nightmares? The teeth in that picture are enough to terrify them."

He folded his arms across his chest and stared at her steadily. "Your diversionary tactic isn't going to work, Rose. You know exactly why you're here."

His shoes made a solid sound on the beautifully polished floorboards as he closed the distance between them. He tilted her chin upward and said in a low tone, "I know who you are, Rose Masterson."

"Of course, I'm Rose Masterson."

He pulled an envelope from the pocket of his leather apron and tapped it in his palm. "This is heavy—far too heavy to hold one thin dollar for that moquette rug."

"I ordered other things, too. My personal expenditures are hardly your concern."

He pinched the thickness of the envelope and stared straight into her eyes. "That rug provided a very clever excuse for you to send an order off to Sears, but the time has come for you to admit that those other things you ordered aren't for you. I strongly suspect this envelope's order contains instructions for—"

"I'm not going to stand here and listen to your cockeyed suppositions, Garret Diamond. When you gave me your word you'd mail that letter, I never dreamed you'd withhold it."

He ignored what she said and traced the two stamps with the blunt edge of his forefinger as he mused aloud, "I've been here long enough to see an interesting pattern. You mail off an order and get something from Sears. Just about the same time, something mysteriously arrives from the Secret Giver for someone in the town."

Maddening man! Why doesn't he tend to his own matters and leave me alone? She lifted her chin. "As often as I order things, you can scarcely consider that a pattern."

When Garret leaned forward, she could smell his bay rum. She'd already felt unbalanced—that heady scent only added to the way her senses whirled.

"You, Rose Masterson, were in the mercantile when Cordelia mentioned her washboard needed to be tacked together again; then she received that washing machine."

"Several other people were in the store at that time, and I knew for a fact that Hugo repaired the washboard very cleverly for her."

He gave a maddening shrug, then started tapping the envelope in his open palm yet again in a nerve wracking beat that matched the much-too-rapid beat of her heart. His voice dropped in volume and tone. "I wonder if Lacey Norse is going to get that new sewing machine she needs to start up her seamstress shop."

Rose's eyes grew wide, and she felt a wave of heat wash over her, but she said nothing.

The corner of his mouth tilted in a smirk, and he gave her a slow, sly wink. She could see the golden shards in his hazel eyes glint with intelligence. "I'm onto your secret."

Flustered, she grabbed the envelope from him and held it behind her back as if that would make this all go away. "Mind your own business."

"I do mind my own business. The good people of Buttonhole seem to think I do a fair job with the mercantile. You, on the other hand, seem to be minding everyone else's business."

"Are you implying I'm a busybody, Mr. Diamond?"

That slow smile widened into a full grin. *Calder's should have used his teeth for their illustration—they're far better looking than the ones on that dreadful poster. Mercy, how could I let my mind wander at a time like this?* Struggling to regain her wits, she inched back from him.

"Yep. I'm saying you've been busy, Miss Masterson. Busy in ways no one but me seems to have detected."

Rose stared at him and tried to think of a way to end the conversation. The problem was, she didn't want to lie. So far, she'd managed to speak the truth each time the subject of the Secret Giver came up. Folks might well have misinterpreted her meaning, but she'd never told a falsehood.

"You may think you figured everything out, Mr. Diamond, but my business is just that—*mine.*

"You minded Mrs. Percopie's business when you bought that fancy icebox for the diner. You minded Joel Creek's business when you bought the plow." Garret didn't give an inch of space or argument. He drew closer again and continued on in a relentless litany. "Mothering might be considered family business, and you sent Mrs. Andrews that layette for the baby she adopted. You set Cordelia up in a laundering business with that high-volume washing machine."

Rose lifted her chin and countered, "I wasn't even living here when the church got the organ."

"I admit, that threw me. Then I recalled you saying you'd visited Buttonhole before you moved here."

She forced a laugh. "Plenty of people pass through town. It could have been any of them."

"It could have been, but it wasn't—" He gave her a stern look. "Was it, Rose? You saw a need, and you took care of it."

"The Secret Giver sent me something, too."

"That was downright clever of you. Diverting attention like that. . ." He shook his head in amazement. "Bet that fooled a few folks, too. You managed to do things like that, and ordering a rifle was a jim-dandy idea. You cooked up mighty interesting ways to keep the curious off your tracks."

Rose fell silent. She'd run out of words, and the exasperating man had her backed into a corner. He'd discovered her precious secret and confronted her. The envelope crackled as she clutched it in her fist. *Now what do I do?*

Garret stepped closer still. "Give me the envelope, Rose. It's time to mail it." He slipped his arm around her and closed his hand around hers.

Clang! The bell sounded as the shop door opened.

eleven

A loud gasp sounded.

Garret kept Rose from bolting by wrapping his other arm around her shoulder and pulling her close. "Mrs. Blanchard. Mrs. Jeffrey," he greeted in an urbane tone that didn't match the thundering heartbeat Rose heard beneath her ear.

"Land o' Goshen!" Mrs. Blanchard blurted out.

"Oh. It's just Rose." Mrs. Jeffrey's tone carried pure relief. "Nothing untoward is happening, Bessie."

"Then what is he doing?"

Garret didn't move hastily. Rose desperately wanted to pull away, but her knees felt too weak, and she realized the wisdom of his actions. Jerking apart would only reinforce something indecent was under way. Instead, Garret kept hold of her.

Good thing, too. The thundering sound filling her ear couldn't possibly be his heart, after all. Rose fought the dizziness that threatened to swamp her.

"I'm afraid I gave Miss Rose a shock, ladies."

"She is pale," Mrs. Jeffrey said. "Look how pale she is."

"Are you okay, Rose? Has something dreadful happened?"

Garret confessed, "I gave her a fright."

"Why, you could scare a body witless, coming down off that ladder. You need to be more careful, young man."

He managed to rob Rose's nerveless fingers of the envelope and scoop her into his arms. Rose tried to make a sound of protest, but he shushed her.

Mrs. Blanchard fumbled in her handbag. "I have those smelling salts in here."

Garret carried Rose to the press-backed oak chair over by the men's boots display. She felt safely anchored in his arms, and when he let go, the mercantile rippled around her once again. "Here you are, Miss Masterson. Sit down and take a few slow, deep breaths to steady yourself."

Mrs. Jeffrey shoved him to the side and muttered, "Give us a moment with her." A few seconds later, Rose felt something yank at her sides and back. Jerking motions. . . What?

"I've loosened her stays," Mrs. Jeffrey whispered. "Can't you find those smelling salts?"

The acrid scent of ammonia and Rose's violent cough answered that question. Rose jerked away from Mrs. Blanchard's vial and gasped.

Garret stood over by the water barrel struggling not to laugh at Rose's predicament. With his back to them, he called out, "Shall I bring over a cool cloth or a dipper of water?"

"Yes. Yes, that would be just the thing," Mrs. Jeffrey said as she smoothed hair back from Rose's face and pinned the loose strands into the bun she now anchored firmly in the correct location.

❧

"Here you are." Garret subtly winked as he handed the cloth to Rose and said with quiet intensity, "Rose, you don't look like yourself right now. I'll stand with you here while the ladies find what they need; then I'll close the store and escort you home to be sure you make it there safely."

"That's unnecessary." Rose tried to stand.

Mrs. Blanchard pressed her back down. "For once, stop acting hale as a horse, Rose. It's only your pride speaking.

Why, I nearly fainted recently, and Mr. Diamond escorted me home, too. It's the gentlemanly thing to do."

Mrs. Jeffrey patted Rose's cheek. "Your color is returning. This is what comes from eating those ridiculous cold cereals for breakfast, Dear. I know you're alone, but you simply must stop shaking that nonsense out of a box, and fix yourself an egg and toast."

"And prunes," Mrs. Blanchard added. "You need to start off your day with wholesome foods. Clearly, your health is slipping."

&

Ten minutes later, with her corset strings and shirtwaist all tucked back into her skirt—thanks to Mrs. Jeffrey's kind assistance—Rose found herself being escorted by Garret toward her house. He'd flatly refused to let her go home alone, and the way he kept hold of her, she would have needed dynamite to blast him from her side.

Completely unsettled, Rose struggled to figure out what to do. Garret had just knocked her whole world off its axis. She wasn't the sort to swoon—was this how women normally felt when they grew faint? Was it because she wasn't accustomed to a man standing so close, or was it this man—who'd just discovered her quiet activities and posed a threat to her secret joy?

"Rosie, we're almost home," he soothed. "Are you feeling any better now?"

Embarrassed and desperately wanting to escape him, she muttered, "I'm perfectly fine, and you're wasting those prunes." She referred to the small box he carried—placed in his hands by Mrs. Blanchard with explicit instructions that Rose needed to have no less than three a day. The thought of eating that sickeningly sweet fruit each day was more than enough cause to make her swoon all over again. She shuddered. "I loathe prunes."

"You're not the only one. They're one of the few fruits I can't stand." He shook the box. "You can give them to Old Hannah the next time you go clean her house." He led her past her ramshackle fence and up toward the house. "Here we are."

She stopped at the threshold and took a stance that would make a suffragette proud. "I'd be lying if I thanked you for bringing me home."

Garret ignored her bravado, opened the door, and nudged her inside. Before she could gather steam, he ordered, "You go put on some tea. We're going to talk."

"Unthinkable." She gave him a wry look. "The good citizens of Buttonhole think I'm dotty, and they're most likely right; but I'm not about to do anything as foolish as inviting you in and risking my reputation and yours."

"You're right. We'll have to be circumspect about our partnership."

"Partnership?" She gawked at him as her stomach somersaulted. Was there no end to the ways this man could find to disturb her? Rose shook her head. "We have no partnership, Mr. Diamond."

He looked into her eyes. "I wouldn't be too sure about that." When he got intense, the gold in his hazel eyes overtook the brown. She'd have to remember that.

"I'll go off to the diner and eat so folks will know I've left you here. I'll sneak back after dark. We'll meet in the backyard by your strawberry barrel."

"You can wait until the crack of doom before I do such a thing."

"You still must not be feeling well. You're not your usual,

cooperative self. Go rest. I'll see you later." He turned and whistled loudly as he left her standing at the door.

Rose fought the urge to slam her door, but she refused to give him the satisfaction of seeing her reaction. *I have to remain calm if I'm going to convince him to— Who am I trying to fool? Garret Diamond is just as stubborn as I am.* She closed her eyes, rested her forehead against the door, and let out a loud, unladylike groan.

ᔌ

Sitting still and dallying over a cup of after-dinner coffee tried Garret's patience. He'd made a point of going to Percopie's Diner immediately after leaving Rose. The incident in the mercantile could have been a catastrophe, and with the way news spread through Buttonhole, folks would be quick to comment if he'd have spent more than just a few moments at Rose's.

"More coffee, Mr. Diamond?"

He glanced up at Hattie, then picked up his cup and tilted it. "I still have half a cup. That'll do. Thanks for asking. You brew a fine pot here."

Hattie scanned the diner. It was early yet—too soon for much of a supper crowd, so she slipped into the chair directly across from him. "Mr. Diamond, I wondered if—well. . ." She sighed and glanced over her shoulder. Her face flushed as she whispered, "I need to ask a favor."

He wondered why she was whispering. "What is it?"

"There's been some talk around town of earning money for a church bell. That always means an auctioned box social." She sighed again. "Please don't be offended, but I—well, I don't want you to bid." Her gaze skittered toward the door, to the kitchen again, then down toward her lap. "Some of the nicest young men in town aren't as well off as you."

Garret took a gulp of coffee. "Anybody I know?"

"Lester Artemis." Her eyes took on a sparkle. "He works at the *Gazette*. He just loves my fried chicken."

"He's a lucky man. I wish you both well."

Hattie popped up from the chair and whispered, "Thank you! Oh—will you please tell Mr. Hepplewhite, too?"

Garret nodded and left the diner, sure he'd wasted sufficient time there. The fact that Hattie spent those few minutes sitting with him certainly helped keep folks from speculating that he'd set his cap for Rose.

He stopped midstride. *Rose. I'm setting my cap for Rose. When did that—how did that happen? The woman has worked her way into my heart, and I'm going to have a real fight trying to turn her affections toward me when I can't even get her to buy stuff from my store!*

As soon as it grew dark and the lamplighter finished his rounds, Garret slipped out of the back door of his place and headed toward Rose's back door. He had to protect her reputation, so he didn't take a direct route. Finally, he reached her house, sneaked around, and tapped lightly on the back door. When she didn't respond, he got irritated. She was trying to ignore him, and he wouldn't put up with it. He rapped more firmly.

Rose finally flung open the door and glowered at him. From the light of the lamp she held, he could see she still wore the same dress she'd had on at his store. Judging from the color in her face, she either had a high fever or a raging temper. "What is all of that racket?"

His own temper flared to life. Vexed that she'd taken her sweet time to answer, he scowled right back. "The crack of doom. Now get out here."

twelve

Her eyes widened at his audacity. "Garret Diamond, I don't know what's come over you, but you're bossy as a war general. I have little patience for anyone who decides to try to run my life."

"Come outside."

"What if I said I'd get too cold out there?" She gave him an exultant smile.

He'd never cross her threshold at night, alone, and she clearly realized it. He wasn't about to let that irritating fact stop him. "It's a balmy night. If you said you'd be cold, you'd be lying. . .and you don't lie. Which is why you didn't deny what I said back at the store." His patience was slipping faster than a skinny man's sleeve garter. "You, Rose Masterson, are the Secret Giver."

Her eyes nearly shot fire at him. "You, Garret Diamond, are a pain in the neck."

He leaned back against the post and chuckled. "Now that we've established our identities, let's negotiate."

She crossed her arms and glowered at him. "Are you trying to blackmail me?"

"Not in the least. What I'm going to do is join you. From here on out, I'm a co-conspirator."

"This isn't funny."

He heard how her voice quavered and realized fear had triggered her temper. "I agree, Rose. This isn't funny; it's important work. It's a ministry."

Some of the fire seemed to leave her eyes. "I still don't think you ought to stick your nose into my business. The sixth chapter of Matthew, verse three says, 'But when thou doest alms, let not thy left hand know what thy right hand doeth.' That being the case, you really do need to stop prying."

He looked through the screen and lowered his tone. "Was it prying when you told me Cordelia Orrick needed that fabric?"

"Of course not."

"So what is the difference if we work together to make life better for our Christian brothers and sisters?"

She rubbed her temples as if he'd given her a terrible headache. "I don't want anyone to know."

"I agree. There isn't any reason for others to know. It'll be a pact between us. I think you've been wise to keep your identity a secret, and you've chosen to give things that equipped others to work and earn for themselves."

Her shoulders drooped as she let out a long, slow sigh of capitulation.

Garret opened the screen door. "Now hand me that lamp, and bring along your precious catalogue. We have work to do."

"It's silly to order from the catalogue anymore. The only reason I did it was to stay anonymous. The things can come from your store now." Her eyes grew glossy, but she blinked away the moisture. "I felt terrible, hurting your feelings by not making some of those purchases from the mercantile."

He reached in, took her hand, and gently tugged her outside. The screen door banged shut. "You were doing it for the right reason."

Rose handed him the lamp and gathered her skirts about

herself as she sat on the uppermost step of the porch. "I was going to get the four-drawer New Queen sewing machine, but I really like the Singer you have at the mercantile much better."

"Then why didn't you plan to order one of those?" He sat beside her and fought the urge to wrap his arm about her shoulders.

"It's not in the catalogue. Oh, don't glower at me. I'm telling the truth." She fished the crumpled envelope from her pocket and smoothed it out on her lap. After taking a deep breath, she tore it open and shook out a small stack of money and her order sheet. "You have plenty of fabric at the mercantile, but I thought it might be nice for her to have some supplies on hand. Often, folks take the material to the seamstress but don't think of all of the notions that go into making a garment."

Garret moved the lamp so he could scan the order sheet more easily. She'd ordered a case of thread, hooks and eyes, Selisia waist lining, buttonhole twist, stays, and lace. Garret set aside the form and took her hand in his. He trailed his fingers across the edge of her cuff. A small, frayed section made him frown.

"Rose, how can you buy all of this for Lacey when you need new gowns yourself?"

She turned her hand so she could inspect the spot he'd touched. Relentlessly, he skipped his fingers along the stained apron pocket, the tattered ribbon trim of her skirt, then up to her collar where he traced the washed-and-worn-until-limp fabric. Very quietly, he stated the fact again. "You need new clothes."

Her nose wrinkled as she took stock of her garments. "Oh,

my. I haven't paid much attention. I really have let myself go. These are shabby, aren't they?"

Soft laughter bubbled out of him. "Rose Masterson, you are so content helping others that you're blind to your own needs. You're the only woman I know who lacks even the smallest scrap of vanity."

"I am content, Garret. Very content. I don't want you to ruin my secret."

He winked at Rose and covered her hand with his. "I'm not going to ruin it; I want to share it. In fact, I'm going to steal a page out of your copybook. We're going to throw everyone off our tracks. Do you have some paste?"

"Yes." She gave him a wary look.

"Good. Get it, a pair of scissors, and this week's *Gazette*."

"What for?"

"You'll see."

In no time at all, they sat side by side with a pair of Rose's serving trays across their laps. Rose leaned over and laughingly added the "orse" she'd cut from the word "horse" after an "N" Garret pasted at an odd tilt. "Good. Now where did the sewing machine go?"

"Here." Rose handed him the little snippet of paper. She'd found it on the back page of the newspaper as they searched for the necessary words.

"Thanks. You know, I ate at the diner, and supper hasn't agreed with me. The chicken was a mite bit greasy." He winced and rubbed his stomach. "Could I trouble you for some bicarbonate?" While Garret continued to paste the rest of the message, Rose went in search of a cure.

By the time she came back outside, he'd started to fold the letter. Garret set it aside and accepted the glass she held out to him. "Thanks, Rose."

She held a plate with bread on it—the bread sparkled in the lamplight. Carefully, she stepped around the trays of paper scraps and scissors and sat beside him. "Bread can help, and so does a little peppermint. My nanny used to make this for me. Try it."

Garret accepted the thick slice of buttered bread that wore a mantle of crushed candy. It smelled yeasty and minty. Just before he took a bite, he raised his brow. "Nanny?"

Rose watched as he chewed. "Nanny." She moistened her lips. "Garret, I've not corrected the folks' assumption in Buttonhole that I'm hard-pressed financially."

"So you have a little nest egg that allows you to do as you will?"

Rose nodded. "So you finished the letter? I want to see it all put together."

He thought about putting her off, but she'd find out soon enough. Garret handed it to her. She leaned to the side a bit to catch more light on the cut-and-paste letter, and her gasp told him she'd read the last line.

"Rose, you just admitted your clothes have grown shabby."

"I can buy or make my own clothes."

He swallowed the last bite of bread. "That's not the point. Other people have noticed the sad condition of what you wear, even if you haven't. To their way of thinking, the Secret Giver would want you to have some new clothes. Hiring the seamstress to do a good deed while buying the sewing machine for her is exactly what everyone would expect, and it'll keep them looking elsewhere for the benefactor."

She gave him a disgruntled look. "You may be right, but I

was right, too. You, Garret Diamond, are a pain in the neck."

❧

The next afternoon, Rose wanted to serve a healthy slice of her mind to her pain-in-the-neck partner. He'd slipped half of the money in her sugar bowl when she wasn't looking, and now he was hustling her into the mercantile. "Garret, I'm busy! You're entirely too commandeering. Can't you see how I need to—?"

He opened the door to the mercantile and announced loudly, "Here she is—show her the note!"

No less than nine chattering women and girls surrounded Rose; all started talking at once, trying to give her the news. Lacey Norse clutched the pasted-together gift letter and wept for joy. Rose didn't have to feign any emotion. It was a touching moment. She glanced over at Garret. He smiled and headed toward the storeroom.

It was turning into quite a pleasant little party. Rose had to smile. All of her lovely friends were celebrating the Secret Giver's wonderful plan to provide Lacey with the much-needed sewing machine while providing Rose with new clothing. They wanted to help choose the fabric and patterns and crowded into the sewing corner of the store.

Mr. Deeter watched from the window of the post office and called out, "Don't you all go fancifying Rose until she's nothing but flounces and froufrou."

Rose laughed. "Simple is best. I have to be able to ride my bicycle."

"This. Just look at this," Leigh Anne's grandma said as she lifted a bolt. "A plaid wool is sensible and stylish for her."

"Grandma, it's summer. Wool is going to be too hot and itchy for her."

Patience Evert sneered at Leigh Anne. "A *lady* wouldn't speak of such things."

Rose smiled at Leigh Anne. "I was about to say exactly what you did, Dearheart. The summer heat can be so oppressive."

"And she got swoony just yesterday," Mrs. Blanchard said.

"I'm perfectly fine," Rose huffed. "It was nothing, I assure you."

"Twaddle." Mrs. Blanchard produced a dark blue muslin. "The only reason you're feeling better is because you ate your prunes this morning. This is practical and will wear well."

"It's a nice shade." Rose reached out to touch it.

"Nonsense. This is a time to cast practicality to the wind and be whimsical." Cordelia lifted a green, water-stained taffeta. "You need a new Sunday-best dress, and this green will do wonders for your eyes."

"Yes, it would," Lacey agreed. "I can just imagine you in it. Mrs. Busby, the ivy print dimity beside you is ideal for a shirtwaist for her."

"And this would make a perfect match for the skirt!" Charity added.

"It would," Rose agreed. "Oh, it's all so very pretty. It's been awhile since I even paid attention to fashion, and these fabrics are marvelous."

"What do you think, Mr. Diamond?" Missy Patterson asked in an adoring tone. "Won't our plain Rose look lovely in it?"

He picked up Pickle and put her in Leigh Anne's lap. Rose secretly wished Garret would like this green. She truly favored it; and since these clothes were his idea, it would be nice if he was pleased with the choices, too.

He cocked his head to one side, then pressed his lips together in a thoughtful line. "Miss Rose will look fine in those. Green suits her—pulls out the green in her graygreen eyes. I confess, though, I'm partial to something. . ." His voice trailed off as he spiraled his hand in the air in a hopeless gesture.

"More feminine," Mrs. Jeffrey filled in. "What about this cotton print?"

Rose was about to admit it was pretty, but Garret jumped right in. "Now that's a good one." He jutted his chin and added, "The flowery one just to the side of it's easy on the eyes, too."

The bell over the shop door clanged. "Shiver me timbers, what's goin' on in here?" Zeb Hepplewhite hobbled into the middle of the store and gawked at everyone.

"The Secret Giver struck again," Garret said.

"He slipped a note under the mercantile door," Lacey said as she pointed to the six-drawer Singer that now held a conspicuous spot in the middle of the store. "I'm getting that wondrous sewing machine!"

"Well how'd ya like that?" Zeb scrunched the side of his face and waved his hand in Rose's direction. "What does that have to do with you all hanging enough bunting off of Rose to make her the grandstand for a picnic?"

"That's the funniest thing I've heard all morning." Rose laughed as she disentangled herself from clinging ivy dimity, sprays of cabbage roses, and clinging mossy green. She paused and fingered the floral that Garret said brought out the green in her eyes. It was one of the prettiest things she'd seen in a long time. "I'm especially fond of this one."

"The Secret Giver wrote that I'm to make Rose three new outfits and. . ."

While Lacey filled Mr. Hepplewhite's ears with the goings-on, Mrs. Blanchard tugged on Rose's sleeve and hissed,

"Don't be mush-mouthed, young woman. You're going to ruin Zebulon's fun if you don't say that a bit louder and let him know just how much you like this piece. Haven't you figured out yet that he's the Secret Giver?"

"Well. . . ," she stammered.

Mrs. Percopie cut in, "No, he's not. It's the banker."

Mrs. Jeffrey shook her head. "No, no. The reverend and I finally figured it out. It's Mr. Deeter."

"The postmaster?" the other two women asked in hushed unison.

Mrs. Jeffrey's head bobbed emphatically. "He was appointed to the position because he comes from good family—one that actually managed to maintain its wealth after the War Between the States. He's been paid a steady salary all of these years from the United States Post Office Department. Besides, from sorting the mail, he knows everybody's business."

Rose glanced over and caught Garret looking at her. A wave of warmth washed over her. She'd never had a man pay attention to her or notice the color of her eyes. Oh, a handful of years ago, there had been a few swains who knew she'd inherit Daddy's fortune. Mere boys, they'd acted like lovesick puppies, and she'd not felt anything but disappointment that they'd seen only the green of dollar bills instead of the green of her eyes. Garret hadn't known about her wealth; he'd simply cared about her.

He winked very slowly, then turned and headed toward a display.

"Isn't that so, Rose?"

"Huh? Oh, I suppose, if you say so." She had no idea what she'd agreed with, but it certainly put a smile on Constance Blanchard's face.

Mrs. Busby muffled a twitter behind her hand. "I declare, Rose, it's a blessing you decided not to marry. If you hadn't noticed that man was better looking than chocolate cake until Constance said so, you simply were intended to be alone."

thirteen

"Mmm-mmm-mmmm." Garret stood at the front door and hummed his appreciation loudly. "Peaches. I don't rightly recall the Good Book saying what heaven smells like, but I declare, this is the scent." He muttered under his breath, "Too bad they don't taste anywhere as good as they smell."

"Let yourself in," Rose called. "I'm busy."

Garret opened the door, and Caramel slinked out and rubbed against his leg. For being the runt of the litter, she'd still managed to thrive under Rose's loving care—but that came as no surprise. Everything and everyone Rose touched flourished.

Garret stepped in, set down the twenty-five-pound bag of granulated sugar, and peeled out of his coat. After hanging the coat on one of the hall tree's hooks, he carried the sugar into the kitchen. "Looks like I'm just in time with this."

Rose didn't turn around. "Please pardon me, but I don't want these to scorch."

"Not to worry. The view's as pleasant as the fragrance." He smiled at the sight of her standing by the stove in her old brown paisley skirt. Damp tendrils curled all around her face and the nape of her neck, and her cheek bore a hectic flush from the heat of the stove. Her apron was askew, and her hips and bustle jostled in cadence with the vigorous way she stirred the pot.

A good four-dozen jars of peaches sat in higgledy-piggledy

rows on the table, and several smaller jars sat in steaming rows. "Just say the word. I'll move the pot for you. In fact, I can hold it and pour the jam directly into the jars if you direct me."

Rose cast a surprised look at him.

He shrugged. "My great-aunts loved to cook, but they were both getting frail enough, they couldn't lift a heavy pot. On more than one occasion, I rolled up my sleeves and helped out."

Minutes later, he curled his hand around sunny yellow crocheted pot holders, hefted the pot, and took it to the waiting jars. In a matter of minutes, he and Rose managed to fill all of them. She hastily wiped the jar mouths clean, popped on the lids, screwed the collars in place, and set them in a water bath to seal them.

"Whew!" She lifted the water dipper for him to take a sip, but he shook his head. After taking a long, cool drink, Rose set it down and smiled. "Thank you for your help. That went much faster and easier."

Garret swiped his forefinger through a blob of jam on the edge of the table and wiped it off on a damp dishcloth. "I'll help with the next batch if you'll give me a jar. I'll send it to my great-aunt Brigit. She'll love it."

"Bite your tongue, Garret. I'm done with peaches for the day. You just feel free to take one of these jars and let me rest."

"From the looks of it, you're done canning for the year. What did you do? Go strip every last peach from the trees?"

"No." She laughed. "This is only a portion of them. I'm going to deliver peaches to Cordelia tonight. Mrs. Kiersty already took a bushel, and she's sending Mr. Hepplewhite for more tomorrow."

He looked at the empty tulip-decorated sugar sack she'd

set aside. "Want to refill your canister before I put this sugar in the pantry?"

"It was generous of you, Garret, but I think you'd better take it back to the store."

"Balderdash." He opened the door to her pantry and stared at the room in shock. "Woman, what—"

"Now, now. You have to understand Sears ships things by weight. I often had them use bags of sugar or flour to bring the weight up to one hundred pounds so the price of freight dropped."

Her so-called pantry was actually a third bedroom. He'd never seen such a collection of things. Speaking aloud, Garret took stock. "Thirty. Forty. Fifty pounds of sugar. Fifty pounds of flour. Beans. My word, you have enough beans in here to feed all of Buttonhole for a month!" He continued to scan the room.

"Maybe Cordelia could use that sugar you brought to me."

He turned and scowled at her. "Maybe Cordelia could come grocery shop here at your house!"

Rose's smile faded. "Cordelia doesn't know about what I keep in there. She's been very careful not to take liberties with my home."

"Why? She's not starchy like some of the other women."

"This was her childhood home."

"You don't say." He felt his unreasoning anger fade. Rose had stocked this room and used most of the contents to make meals for Old Hannah, soups and teas for Mrs. Kiersty and the boardinghouse folks, countless lunches and suppers for Hugo and Prentice. . . .

Rose turned back toward the kitchen. She cut a fresh loaf of bread, took the slice, and sopped it in the bottom of the jam pot. When she held that treat out to him, Garret covered her fingers and gently pushed it back toward her mouth. "You have it. I'll take the heel."

"No." She grinned. "I feed the heels to the birds."

"Woman, you never cease to amaze me. You can find something nice to do for anyone or anything."

"I've had nice all my life. There's nothing wrong with me making sure others have a turn at it, too." She cut a slice and handed it to him.

As he slowly pretended to dredge his own slice, yet soaked up no more than a speck of the still-warm jam that lined the pot, he asked, "What's our next Secret Giver project going to be?"

"Shirts, I think. Mary Ellen used to sew all of Hugo's shirts. He's nearly worn them out, and he's not gotten a new shirt since she passed on."

Jealousy stabbed at Garret for a moment. Rose did Hugo's laundry every week. Indeed, Garret had seen Hugo stringing up a new clothesline for her just last Sunday. Hugo relied on Rose for meals, laundry, and baby-sitting. With all of those essentials met, Hugo did nothing more than fill Rose's stove and lamps and made sure she had firewood. Hugo didn't seem like the type to take advantage of a woman's sweet and generous heart, so that meant he must be biding his time before he convinced Rose that Prentice shouldn't be a motherless boy. That argument would hold a lot of sway.

Garret barely tasted the dot of jam on the bread that he shoved in his mouth. Two chews, and he swallowed as he scowled. "It occurs to me that you wash, mend, and iron Hugo's shirts. The least he could have done is mend your fence."

"I wouldn't want him to."

"That's beside the point." He took a quick glance out at the fence. Caramel leapt up on it at that moment, and even the kitten's slight weight made the rickety fence wobble. Garret looked back at Rose and demanded, "Has he ever offered?"

"No." She gave a small shrug and nibbled on her bread.

He wiped his hands off on a damp towel. "Well, I'm going to see to it that your fence is repaired. It's an eyesore."

"No!" Rose shook her head adamantly. "Leave my fence alone."

"Tell me why, Rose." He folded his arms across his chest and waited.

Rose stared straight back at him, her graygreen eyes sparkling with defiance. Her hairpins must have come loose as she shook her head. A few pinged onto the floor, and her not-quite-on-the-top topknot started to uncoil. Hectic color filled her cheeks, and she reached up to keep her hair from coming down. Realizing she still held the jam-covered heel of bread, she halted the movement.

Garret froze, too. He'd love to see her hair flowing over her shoulders. Her blush made him do the gallant thing. "Allow me to help." He hastily collected the pins he could find and stood behind her. She shifted uneasily. "Being antsy and fidgeting is making it come down. Hold still, Rosie."

Garret tucked the pins between his lips and gazed at the ever-loosening honey blond mane. The tiny tendrils at her nape weren't damp anymore, he noticed.

Soft. Her hair felt incredibly soft. He knew he ought to simply try to crank it back into a tighter twist and jam in those pins. As soon as he did, she could wash her hands, excuse herself, and go make herself presentable again.

Instead, he held the bulk of it in his left hand. Tresses spilled from his grasp in a warm, satiny fall that went past her hips. Rose shivered and let her bread drop into the sink as she curled her hands around the edge of the counter.

Garret took a steadying breath and finger-combed the portions by her temples and forehead back into his hand with the rest. At first, he started to twist the abundant mass counterclockwise, then changed his mind and went the opposite direction.

Rose inched to the side a bit, her movement nervous. She turned as much as she could and looked at him from the corner of her eye, over her shoulder. He could see vulnerability in her expression that he'd not seen before. She usually looked so self-assured and carefree. This was a different side of her— unguarded, unsure. "You needn't fuss, Garret," she whispered unsteadily. "Just—"

"Seems to me," he said around the pins in his most soothing tone, "you're the one who's fussing, Rose. Your hair is glorious."

He'd never dressed a woman's hair. Never wanted to—until now. At least twenty different shades of honey, wheat, and gold shimmered in his hands. From having been twisted so tightly together, the strands still hung in a long loose spiral. As he twisted them and coiled the length back onto her crown, Garret knew he wasn't arranging it as she would have. Rose always crammed it tightly into a knot that would fit in a stingy teacup; he'd eased it into a. . .a delicious cinnamon roll-like coil that took his entire hand span to keep in place as he anchored it with the pins.

Lazily putting the pins in and resituating them so they'd hold, he asked, "Why wouldn't you want me to fix your fence, Rose? You're always willing to help others; I'd love to help you."

"It isn't that," she said quietly.

"Then what's the problem?"

"Cordelia needs it the way it is."

He only had two hairpins left. He paused before choosing where to put them. "What does Cordelia have to do with it?"

Rose started to turn around. He wouldn't let her.

She sighed. "I told you this was her home. Not long after I moved in, I went out to cut down the morning glory, take down the fence, and replace it. Admittedly, it's in terrible condition. Cordelia was taking a constitutional, and she stopped to chat. One morning, her beau came by and took her for a walk. He picked a morning glory from the vine, and she started to apologize for it being there. It's a weed, you know."

"Yes, but a pretty one."

"Jonathan told her it was called bindweed. He professed his love and proposed to her there by the fence. He said she'd twined her way into his heart, and he wanted her bound there forever."

Garret placed the last hairpin, took Rose by the shoulders, and turned her around. Tears turned the gray shards of her eyes silver. She blinked away the dampness.

"How could I be so selfish as to destroy something that gives a lonely widow such comfort?"

Garret studied her quietly, then murmured, "Of course you couldn't, Rose."

Tempted to pull her into his arms, Garret cleared his throat. "I need to get going. I just wanted to drop off that sugar."

"I'll bring you some peaches and jam tomorrow. You'd burn yourself on the jars right now."

"Fine." As he headed toward the door, she turned toward

the other portion of the house. Garret shut the door and shook his head. He'd been so caught up in paying attention to Rose, he'd forgotten the sugar. Oh, well. It didn't much matter. She'd undoubtedly use it somehow.

He turned and saw Hugo standing by the sagging, peeling fence and nodded. "Lassiter."

"Diamond." Hugo still wore the brown suit he'd worn to work at the bank, but now the coat was unbuttoned. He glanced at his pocket watch meaningfully, then closed it and tucked it back in his vest pocket.

The action rated as utterly ridiculous. Businesses were closed for the evening, but with it being late spring, the sun hadn't even set. *Rosa always says Hugo is just a friend and neighbor, but she's sure that's all I am, too. This isn't the first time I've suspected he's sweet on her. Well, too bad. She's mine.*

Garret strode toward him.

"Rose isn't exactly mindful of appearances," Hugo started in.

"She doesn't need to be. She's beautiful just the way she is." Garret didn't hesitate for a moment to speak his mind. Hugo had been looking at his watch—well, he might as well learn what time it was. Time for him to turn around, go home, and mind his own affairs. "Anybody who thinks otherwise is both blind and heartless."

Hugo chuckled and raised both hands in a gesture of surrender. "You don't need to convince me. I wasn't referring to her looks, though. I'm pointing out that it's not proper for a man and woman to be—"

Garret bristled. "Are you intimating that Miss Masterson and I have conducted ourselves—?"

"No. Absolutely not." An all-too-entertained smile lit Hugo's face. "Miss Rose is so dead-set on staying single, she'd be oblivious if a gentleman came calling with candy and flowers."

"And you'd know that because you've tried?" Garret rasped.

"Nope. Rose is like a sister—any affection I hold for her is purely fraternal. You, on the other hand, seem to be getting a mite possessive."

Relieved at Hugo's words and more than ready to stake his claim, Garret stared him straight in the eye. "Yep. I am."

"So that's the way of it." Hugo's smile grew wider still. "Truth be told, I have my eye on Cordelia Orrick. Hired her to start doing my laundry. It made for a good excuse to go on over to her place."

"She's a fine woman." Garret didn't bother to hide his grin. Things were turning out even better than he'd dared to hope.

"Nice little daughters, too. They get along with Prentice just fine. I don't think it'll take long before I can pop the question." Hugo gave him an amused look. "Convincing Rose is going to take some doing on your part."

"I'm equal to the task."

Hugo seemed to think about it for a minute, then nodded slowly. "I can believe it." He extended his hand. "I'm not above scheming if it'll result in her being happy. Let me know if I can help you out."

Garret shook hands with him. "Thanks."

fourteen

The next day, Rose sauntered toward the mercantile with two jars of peaches and another two of peach jam. The afternoon sun felt wonderful on her cheeks. Of course, that meant she'd forgotten to wear her hat again, but feeling heaven's warm kiss was worth more than bowing to silly rules about fashion.

She could hear Garret and Prentice before she opened the door. Unwilling to spoil the moment with the clang of the bell, she walked around to the back of the mercantile and sneaked in. Pickle scampered past as she tiptoed across the storeroom floor, but Rose tried to determine where they were. The curtains were open just a crack, and she shifted to peek through.

Prentice sat cross-legged on the counter, and Garret perched alongside him, his long legs dangling. His right foot tapped in the air to keep beat as they played a duet of "Shoo Fly" on their harmonicas. As soon as they finished, Prentice begged, "Again!"

"That was four times in a row, Buster. I'm going to run out of breath."

Unwilling to be an eavesdropper, Rose set down the jars and clapped as she walked through the curtains, into the store. "*I'm* breathless. That was a wonderful performance."

Prentice shoved his glasses higher on his nose. "You don't sound all squeaky and barky like the Sneedly kids do when they can't breathe."

Garret chuckled. "Rose, Doc tells me those kids are doing better."

"Praise the Lord, they are."

"Miss Rose makes ever'body feel better." Prentice blew a few notes on his harmonica, then added, "Doc says the herbs she gives him from her yard keep Mr. Ramsey's heart going, and Daddy says she's the onliest one around who can make Mr. Van der Horn smile."

"Now that's really saying a mouthful." Garret tucked his harmonica into his shirt pocket and reached for the jar of licorice. "I reckon I'd best get back to work now. Why don't each of you have a treat?"

"Wow!"

"Prentice, mind your manners," Rose chided softly.

"Thanks, Mr. Diamond!" Prentice took the licorice stick and scrambled down from the counter.

Rose caught the ball of string Garret used to tie up packages as it went flying. As she got ready to put it back on the counter, it felt odd. She glanced down and groaned at the bedraggled shape it was in. "Pickle?"

"Yep." Garret shrugged. "It's a definite improvement over the pickle jar. At least string doesn't leave her smelling funny for days on end. Did you come for any particular reason?"

From the way he glanced at Prentice, Rose couldn't be sure whether Garret was asking whether she'd come to fetch the boy or whether he was reminding her they had an audience so she shouldn't say anything about the Secret Giver.

"I need some cheesecloth and wire-mesh screen. Do you have any?"

"What will you be using them for?"

She walked past him, around the counter, and into the mercantile. "I fear I've used my Peerless food dehydrator so much, the screens on it are giving out in protest."

"And we're gonna make dried 'cots," Prentice informed Garret. "Miss Rose washes them, and I twist 'em in half. Only I don't spit out the pits."

"I'd hope not." Garret went to the hardware section and located the proper mesh. "A gentleman should never spit in the presence of a lady."

"Lotsa men chaw and spit." Prentice wiggled and bumped into the door. "It's yucky."

"Prentice, please prop open the door. It would be nice to have a breeze come through." Garret redirected his attention to Rose. "This mesh is thirty inches wide. How much do you need?"

"Five yards of each, please."

Garret leaned back and gawked. "Five yards?"

"Yes, please."

"Oh, now isn't that simply splendid!" Mrs. Kiersty stood in the open door and beamed. "Rose, I wondered if the day would ever come."

"What day?" Rose and Garret asked in unison.

"What's happening?" Mr. Appleby slipped past Mrs. Kiersty and entered the mercantile.

"Rose is buying five yards of fabric—and not one kind, but two! Two, mind you. She's decided it's time to—"

"Excuse me, Mrs. Kiersty, but I'm not buying fabric. I'm buying mesh so I can make dried fruit and fruit leathers."

"Oh." Mrs. Kiersty looked entirely too dejected by that revelation.

Mr. Sibony, on the other hand, perked up. "You do have a way with those. I remember the strawberries you dried last year. The missus and I sure relished them when you left them behind that day you came to help her with the darning."

"Darning?" Garret's brow wrinkled, then softened as he smiled. He stooped, lifted Pickle, and absently petted him.

"Mrs. Sibony broke her arm last winter." Rose smiled at Mr. Sibony. "It healed up, good as new. She showed me that quilt she's piecing. The colors in it are beautiful."

"Well since we're talking about material. . ." Mrs. Kiersty tugged on the cuff of her glove. "I still think Rose ought to buy some and make a dress for herself."

"Nonsense." Rose walked over and took the mesh from Garret. "Everyone knows the Secret Giver provided a very generous new wardrobe for me."

"Then why aren't you wearing one of those new skirts?" Mrs. Kiersty scowled at Rose's old cream-and-green-striped dress.

"I'm spending the day in my kitchen, preserving fruit. It would be impractical for me to wear nice clothing, and I'd be mortified to offend someone by ruining those pretty new dresses with sticky sap and juice."

"I've decided who that someone is." Mr. Sibony's voice dropped. "Mr. Milner—he's the Secret Giver. I'm sure of it."

"How did you reason that out?" Garret took the mesh back from Rose. He winked at her as he did so. "Five yards?"

"Yes, please."

Mr. Sibony and Mrs. Kiersty accompanied them over to

the cutting table. Mr. Sibony said, "Hank Milner got that inheritance—remember?"

Mrs. Kiersty's head bobbed.

"It was just before you moved to Buttonhole, Rose." Mr. Sibony nodded his head emphatically. "The timing is just right. He's the one."

Garret cut the mesh and began to roll it up. "I'm still meeting folks in town. Other than shaking Mr. Milner's hand at church, I haven't spoken with him. Mrs. Milner seems like a kindhearted woman, though."

"Oh, she is." Rose had to restrain herself from grabbing the mesh and running out the door. These situations were dreadfully uncomfortable. She refused to lie, but this time she hadn't needed to even hedge because of how cleverly Garret managed to turn the conversation. "I've heard she's organizing the bazaar so the church can raise money for a steeple bell."

"That'll be a lot of work." Garret snipped a length of string off the battered ball and tied the mesh into a tidy scroll. "But it's for an excellent cause. If there's a committee, I could volunteer to help out. One of the blessings of being single is that I'm free to use my spare time however I wish."

"Rose says the same thing." Mrs. Kiersty sighed. "Well, I can't spend all day jawing. I have hungry boarders to feed, and I'm clean out of baking soda and running low on lard and salt. If I don't have biscuits, pie, or cookies, we're likely to have a riot over there at supper."

"Seems to me, Zeb wouldn't allow anyone to bother you." Garret drummed his fingers on the tabletop. "He's a quick-thinking man."

"Quick thinking, but not quick moving." Mrs. Kiersty called over her shoulder as she headed toward the shelf with the baking ingredients on it. "His gout's making him miserable again. Actually, his misery is making *me* miserable. The man sits there all day, grumping and groaning about his feet, of all things. Feet! That kind of talk in a kitchen is enough to turn a body's stomach."

"Speaking of feet—I came in for about fifteen feet of chicken wire." Mr. Sibony shoved his hands in his pockets. "The missus says she thinks we have 'bout enough store credit from her eggs to cover it."

"Eggs are twenty-two cents a dozen, and you folks have fine laying hens. I wouldn't be surprised at all if you had gracious plenty. Let me check."

Garret nodded, then reached for the credit ledger. Suddenly, he turned, stooped, and rose with the jars in his hands. A slow smile lit his face. "Rose, I can't believe you brought all of this. Why don't you take some of this jam over to Old Hannah while I see to Mr. Sibony and Mrs. Kiersty?"

"I already took her some." Rose figured he was trying to get rid of her so he could discuss the Sibony's financial situation in private. "I did hear Wilbur Grim's ailing."

Mrs. Kiersty gasped. "Rose Masterson, you have no business paying that man a visit!"

"He's the town drunk," Mr. Sibony whispered to Garret in a confidential tone.

Rose felt Garret's gaze. She stared straight back at him. "He lost a limb in the War Between the States, and he's bitter. But he has never once been hostile to me, and he has a twelve-year-old son, Aaron. Aaron and Trevor were here last Monday, playing draughts with Leigh Anne."

"Oh. I somehow got the notion he was Trevor's brother."

"Coulda been." Mr. Sibony chuckled. "The Kendricks have a sizable brood—I can't keep 'em all straight, and I grew up in Buttonhole."

"This can't be right." Mr. Deeter's exclamation startled them all. He stood up behind the barred window in the post office and shook his finger at Garret. "You gave me your word that if you ordered anything heavy through the post office, you'd give me fair warning."

"I did agree, and I've kept my word." Garret gave him a baffled look.

"I just got a note that says you've got a huge crate, heavy 'nuff to take a full team to pull, waiting at the train."

Garret shook his head. "I have a shipment due in on Friday, but I plan to pick it up. It'll be several boxes—but nothing heavy or large. There must be some mistake."

Mr. Sibony scratched his arm. "I've got me my wagon and team hitched outside."

Garret tugged at the garter on his sleeve. "You might end up with credit enough for that chicken wire and more. Mrs. Kiersty, I'll just put the baking soda and lard on the boardinghouse's tab."

"I can scrape together enough to get by until tomorrow. Let's go see what came!"

"I'll need to sign for the delivery." Mr. Deeter came around, locked the door to the post office, and they all traipsed out of the mercantile. Garret flipped over a "closed" sign and locked the door while Mr. Sibony unhobbled his lead horse.

Garret curled his hands around Rose's waist so he could lift her up into the wagon bed. He drew her a bit closer, squeezed, and murmured under his breath, "What have you done this time, Rose?"

She just laughed.

fifteen

"This thing weighs half a ton," Garret grunted as he and the other men shoved the crate into a space he'd cleared in the mercantile. Half of Buttonhole's citizens had gotten involved. They all stared at the crate with great anticipation.

"Let's open 'er up," Mr. Deeter said.

Garret grabbed a crowbar and carefully pried off the crate's lid. Everyone leaned forward, only to sigh in dismay. "Lots of packing straw," he said aloud. "I'll have to open the front."

"You're testing my patience, young man." Mrs. Kiersty took off her glasses and waggled them at him until her hat bounced from the emphatic action. "You're purposefully trying to string this out, and my old heart can't take it."

"Are you expecting something, Mrs. Kiersty?" Rose asked softly.

"Nothing but heart failure if he doesn't hurry up," the woman confessed in a sheepish mutter. "I feel like a guest at a birthday party. The gift is his, but I'm excited as can be for him!"

Nails screeched as Garret pried the crate open. He loosened one side, then the other. He looked at Mr. Sibony. "How about if you yank on that side, and I'll get this one?"

"Thought you'd never ask."

The huge front panel made a loud crash as it hit the floor. Bits of straw fluttered in the air like confetti. Garret brushed off more of the packing and uncovered bright blue cloth.

"Well, what is it?" Mr. Deeter impatiently reached in and

dusted off more on one end. "Material? Material can't be this heavy."

Garret spied an envelope. He snatched it and pivoted around. "Rose, why don't you open this and read it for us?"

"If you insist." She waved him back toward the contents. "You go on ahead and unload."

If he didn't know for a fact that she was behind this, Garret would never suspect that Rose had anything at all to do with it. She waved at him again. "Hurry. I want to see!"

As the men pulled the heavy fabric from the box, she read aloud, "Instructions for installing your awning. Well, what do you think of that? Your emporium is going to have the prettiest blue awning the people of Buttonhole have ever seen."

"We all expected great things from you when you came to town, Diamond." Mr. Deeter slapped him on the back.

Removing the fabric caused more of the packing straw to sift and fall, revealing not just the necessary metal ribs and posts to support the awning, but also wrought iron. "This is too much."

"It is wonderful," Mrs. Kiersty gushed. "Don't you think so, Rose?"

"I think those benches will look perfect out front." Rose shoved the instructions back into Garret's hands. "Let's all work together and put them there right away."

The men crowded around, grabbed hold of the heavy pieces, and carried them back outside. Mrs. Kiersty, in her bossiest tone, made sure the men centered each bench beneath the windows on either side of the door. Garret stared at the custom benches in awestruck silence.

The glossy black metal didn't carry the usual curlicues or

floral designs. A low arc crowned the back with a circle in the center containing a diamond shape. Two thick solid bands with diamond shapes were at the top and bottom of the back, with "DIAMOND'S EMPORIUM" metal lettering filling in the middle section. The diamond-in-a-circle motif formed the seat, arms, and legs of both of the seven-foot-long benches.

"Son," Zeb Hepplewhite said as he hobbled over, "you're not gonna be able to move those things again. To my way of thinking, you're stuck in Buttonhole for life."

"He's not just stuck here; he's volunteered to help out." Mr. Sibony turned to Mrs. Milner. "He said he'll help you with the church bazaar so we can finally get that steeple bell."

Garret nodded. He was listening, but most of his thoughts centered on something other than the bell. Stinging from the fact that Rose considered him in need of such an act of charity, he decided he'd have to sit her down and explain a few facts—the first of which was, he was in stable financial condition. He had become her partner so they could have a ministry of giving. Receiving was out of the question—well, he corrected himself, she needed those clothes Lacey Norse made, and wearing them was an act of kindness because Rose made for a beautiful advertisement.

He kept looking at Rose. She'd made sure Leigh Anne got to sit on the bench first, and when Mrs. Jeffrey stopped her to say something, Rose gave her a quick hug and nodded. She and the town had a rare affinity for one another. Sweet, wild Rose. She'd cultivated a family for herself here, and her roots went down deep.

Rose sat down on the other bench, and Prentice hopped up and wiggled until he was plastered to her side. She curled her arm around his shoulders and laughed as Mrs. Altwell and her children joined them.

"Mr. Diamond!" Rose called merrily. She leaned forward to glance over at the other bench, which held a full load of citizens. "Look at this. Just look! I think the Secret Giver might be allowing your fine mercantile a bit of advertising here, but I'm sure he must have intended these benches as a gift for everyone in town. Why, the only thing that's going to improve this is that awning. Surely, this is a fine day for Buttonhole!"

Garret felt the knot inside of him untie at her sweet words. Dear Rosie—she'd just turned the tables on him. He'd been thinking of the selfsame excuse of advertising as a way to give her clothing. Everyone on the benches chattered happily, but Rose—well, she positively glowed with joy. He couldn't very well spoil her happiness by fostering foolish pride.

"The woman's right, you know," the banker agreed. "Buttonhole's folks do need a place to rest now and then."

"I'd have to say, there's no better town than Buttonhole." Garret nodded, then turned to Mrs. Milner. "I have a few ideas for the bazaar. Have you set a date?"

"Hugo Lassiter said he could meet tonight. Cordelia Orrick can watch his little boy for him."

"Fine." He saw Rose directing Trevor and Adam as they carried the wooden panels from the crate out of the store. "Hey! Wait a minute. We're going to need those for a booth for the bazaar."

"Why, yes. Waste not, want not," Mrs. Milner said.

Garret dropped his tone. "It's for a kissing booth."

Mrs. Milner squealed.

"Ma'am?" He wondered if he'd offended her with that plan.

Clapping her gloved hands, Mrs. Milner called out, "Everyone listen! We're having something different this year for the church bazaar—something perfectly scandalous." Her eyes sparkled with glee. "Mr. Diamond is going to build a kissing booth!"

"Diamond, you're going to kiss the women?" Joel Creek teased.

Garret tapped his foot on the hard-packed street. "Nope. All of Buttonhole's pretty maids are going to pucker up."

"I don't know if I want my daughters doing such a thing," Lula Mae spluttered.

"It's harmless fun." Rose patted her arm. "And just think—you'll want the steeple to have a bell to peal on their wedding days."

"Did you all hear that? Miss Masterson has given her approval." Garret grinned. "We'll all make sure she sets a good example and spends some time in the booth."

sixteen

Rose paused at her hall tree before she left the house. The beveled mirror reflected her new floral dress. Lacey had done a lovely job sewing it. Rose glanced up and caught sight of her hair. "I look a fright," she said to herself as she tried in vain to reposition some of her pins to make the bun look fashionably soft and secure.

"Oh!" she finally said in exasperation. She snatched her straw hat off a hook and slapped it on her head. That ought to do. It even made her presentable—not that such a thing ought to matter. She simply needed to go buy a few yards of ribbon and lace so she could pretty up the jars she'd canned for the bazaar. Well, at least that was her excuse. She needed to ask Garret a few things, but their partnership required that she concoct reasons to visit the mercantile.

They'd been stealing a moment here and there to pray together, seeking wisdom and guidance on how the Lord would have them meet the needs in their community. God had been faithful. Just last week, Garret showed her a trunkful of merchandise he'd found in the store's attic that included a sturdy toolbox with a beginner's assortment of tools. She'd come up with the thought that Aaron Grim could be paid if he helped construct booths for the bazaar.

On an afternoon when Cordelia managed the store, Garret went through the merchandise and decided what he ought to sell and what the Secret Giver should send to someone. Garret told Rose to come with a list of needs; he'd made a list of goods. Truly, God's hand was on them. The lists were a perfect match.

Rose smiled at the benches on her way into the store. They'd turned out even better than she'd dared hope. Garret had been fit to be tied with her at first, opening that big crate. At that moment, it dawned on her that she might have stepped amiss and hurt his feelings.

The warmhearted smile he'd given her when he finally calmed down and agreed that the benches were really for the townspeople meant the world to her. He understood the gift wasn't for him alone. Yes, he'd been able to see the truth and accept it with grace. With the shade from the awning covering the benches, folks could rest and visit before or after they spent time in his wonderful emporium.

The door opened, and Mrs. Blanchard smiled. "Rose! Are you ready for tomorrow?"

"Not yet. I have to get a bit of lace and ribbon to put around my jars of peaches."

Mrs. Blanchard backed into the store and drew Rose in along with her. "Dear, you need to use a bit of lace and ribbon on yourself. We'll fix you up for the kissing booth!"

Rose laughed. "Garret was just teasing me. I'm not going to actually spend time at the booth. We want to make money for the bell. Missy, Hattie, Patience—"

"Piffle!" Mrs. Blanchard towed her toward the colorful array of ribbons. "Dear, many a man would be happy to part with a few cents to get a peck from you. Isn't that right, Mr. Diamond?"

Rose turned and smiled at him. He must have just gotten back from the barbershop. His hair looked a bit shorter and was freshly treated with Brilliantine, and she caught a whiff of bay rum—the heady, masculine scent she'd come to associate with him.

He studied her from hat to hem, and Rose suddenly felt her amusement change to. . .anxiety.

"Don't answer her, Garret. I'm far too old to play such games."

"Rose, Rose, Rose." He shook his head. "I'm not about to let you demure. We've all heard of 'putting your money where your mouth is.' You'll be lending your mouth, Rose, and the men of Buttonhole will be donating their money."

"I'm going to be busy enough already. I'm helping at the cakewalk, and I promised Old Hannah I'd wheel her over so she could look at the quilt and crochet booth."

"I'll take your shift at the cakewalk." Cordelia smiled, and her cheeks filled with color as she averted her gaze. "I was going to ask you if you'd mind. I'd count it a favor."

Mrs. Blanchard whispered, "Mr. Lassiter is working the cakewalk, isn't he?"

Rose felt disoriented. *How could I have missed that? Hugo's started taking his laundry to Cordelia, and she watched Prentice when he went to the planning meetings for the bazaar. Why, they're sweet on each other!*

Garret grinned smugly. "There you have it! Cordelia will do the cakewalk, and you can do the kissing booth. I'm certainly planning on getting my two cents' worth!"

The next day, Rose watched as Missy Patterson left the kissing booth with a jar full of coins to take to the counting table. Hattie Percopie, dressed in a fetching lavender organdy dress, stepped into the booth. Folks laughed as Lester Artemis hopped right up to be first in line. As soon as he paid his two cents and got a kiss, he went straight to the back of the line to get another.

Young love. That's what it was. Rose smiled at the sight, then headed toward the edge of the park so she could go get Old Hannah. She stopped by the counting table where the mayor and pastor sat side by side, drinking Hire's root beer that the bank had donated. Leigh Anne sat under a big, candy-striped, lawn umbrella. A sign in the grass next to her featured an outline of a bell. Thin horizontal lines had been penciled in, and when that sum of money had been raised, she'd color in the corresponding segment.

Rose arrived at Old Hannah's home, only to find Mrs. Jeffrey and Mrs. Busby there already. They all fussed over Buttonhole's oldest citizen, then turned on Rose.

"I'm so glad to see you wore that dress. It's so very feminine," Mrs. Busby gushed. "The green positively matches your eyes, and the sash—well, nearly every woman I know would nearly perish to have such a tiny waist to show off like that."

"I brought my rose petal paper," Mrs. Jeffrey chimed in as she pulled it from her pocket. "A tiny bit of this will put a little more color in your cheeks." She nudged Rose into a chair and applied the tint.

"Bite your lips so they'll redden up a tad, too," Mrs. Busby insisted. "See? You look fresh as a flower. Wonderful! Just wonderful."

"Blushing and bloody—now there's a face that will scare away any male from knee pants on up." Rose tried to inject a touch of humor to her voice. Secretly, she still hoped to avoid the kissing booth.

She'd endorsed Garret's vaguely scandalous plan for the booth because she knew the men in Buttonhole were gentlemen and wouldn't behave in an unseemly way toward the young ladies who took a turn. Still, she hadn't imagined Garret would rope her into serving a spell in the booth! Why, she was five and twenty—no longer young and dewy, but a spinster. The men would want to spend their two cents for a kiss from a pretty young woman at the first blush of her womanhood. Rose was well past her prime, and it would be humiliating to have only one or two gallant men pity her and pay for kisses they did not want. She'd rather spare them—and herself—the embarrassment.

From the looks of how the young ladies were doing when she left the bazaar to come here, Garret's idea was garnering a healthy addition to the funds. Combined with foods, toys, quilts, and several other moneymaking venues and ventures, Buttonhole stood a fair chance of amassing enough to fund the much-longed-for bell. Rose figured if she merely lagged and dallied, Buttonhole would reach the goal. Leigh Anne would color in the last line on the bell, making it unnecessary for Rose to take a turn in the kissing booth.

Hannah's son showed up and whistled at his mother. "I'm going to have to beat back the old gents all day. You're glowing like a young girl."

"And how about Rose?" Mrs. Jeffrey prompted.

"I'll help him beat back the old gents," Rose volunteered.

"You'll be busy at the kissing booth," he countered. "In

fact, I mentioned to Mrs. Milner that I was coming back to get Mother, and she said Patience Evert is balking."

"Bless her heart, Lula Mae has her hands full with that one." Mrs. Busby shook her head.

"Well, Rose is to run on ahead and take her turn in the booth. Mother, I'll take you, and Rose can show you the quilts and such later."

Rose couldn't quite figure out how they managed it. Mrs. Jeffrey and Mrs. Busby each took her by an arm and hustled her toward the park. She didn't have a chance to protest. Hattie Percopie stood in the kissing booth, her penny jar half-full, and Lester Artemis was turning his pockets out to scrounge up another two cents.

"Lester, why don't you escort Hattie over to the counting table?" Mrs. Jeffrey didn't bother to hide her smile behind her gloved hand. "It looks to me that the reverend and the mayor will have plenty to add to the bell fund, Hattie."

Mrs. Milner and Garret walked up. Garret wore his Sunday-best suit and a natty new straw hat, which he gallantly swept off. "Ladies."

"Good, you're here, Rose." The strain around Mrs. Milner's eyes eased. "We can't have the kissing booth go empty—it's the biggest success I've ever seen!"

"I'll ruin that record." Rose eyed the booth with trepidation. Garret and Aaron had built it, using the wood from the benches and awning. "It's a grand booth, though."

"Charity and Mrs. Kiersty made the bunting." Garret reached over and tugged her away from the safety of standing between the other women. "Now it's your turn to do your part."

"Garret, I really don't think—"

"You're not here to think, Rosie. You're here to pucker."

He took a jar from a shelf he'd cleverly built inside the booth and thumped it down in plain view on the ledge, then sauntered off.

Plink, plink. Pennies fell into the jar. Rose turned in surprise to see who would waste two cents to kiss a spinster.

seventeen

"Hi, Miss Rose!"

"Prentice." She let out a sigh of relief. She'd never been kissed before—well, other than by a child or her parents. This would be simple enough.

Hugo held Prentice a bit higher, but Prentice wouldn't stop wiggling until he knelt on the ledge and grabbed hold of her shoulders. "I earned my pennies by playing my ha'mon'ca for Daddy."

"I'm honored."

She accepted Prentice's kiss and gave him a hug. Hugo helped him down, then dropped a dime along with his two cents into the jar. Rose opened her mouth to tell him, but he shook his head. "Rose, there's two cents there for me, then the rest is for my son, Cordelia, and her daughters. We're all thankful to you for your kindness and friendship." He brushed a kiss on her cheek.

"Hey, now, what is that?" Zeb reached up and did his sleight-of-hand trick. He pulled a quarter from behind her ear, gave it a surprised look, then dropped it in the jar. "Rose, my girl, never had me a daughter, but I like to imagine if I did, she'd a' been like you." He puckered up and gave her a fatherly kiss.

Rose could scarcely imagine the sweet things those men had told her. They warmed her heart and made her glad Garret had forced her into this booth, after all. She looked out and gasped. A line of Buttonhole's males trailed around the edge of the park. Young and old, married and single, rich and poor—the men were all lined up to kiss her!

"Took us a minute to recognize you, Miss Masterson," Mr. Deeter called out. "Take off that-there hat so we can see the sun shine on your hair and know it's really our Rose."

All of the old fears eased: *Don't fidget, Rose. A proper lady. . . The mannerly thing. . . People of our social station. . . Be sure to. . . Never. . . Always. . . Mind your posture, Dear. . .* The stuffy rules of society, the pretentious code of behavior, the impossible strictures swirled in her mind. Mama and Papa had been gentle, but persistent, in her guidance. When her parents passed on, though, the rules nearly stifled Rose. Unwilling to spend her lifetime steeped in artifice, she'd sought out a place where others wouldn't inconvenience her if she stepped awry while, as Thoreau would say, she kept pace with a different drummer. She'd chosen Buttonhole and found happiness here. Here, she could be herself—she could love others and be loved just for herself instead of her bank account or social status.

Jesus, thank You for this. My heart is so full!

Overcome with joy, she took off her hat and flung it into the air. It sailed over the park, landed in a tree, and sent several birds into flight. She clapped in delight as the men cheered.

Aaron Grim paid two cents—hard-earned money he couldn't afford—to give her a kiss. "You always treat me like I'm somebody instead of a drunk's boy. I'm gonna be somebody someday, Miss Rose. I'll make you proud."

"You're already somebody special, Aaron. I'm already proud to know you."

Trevor Kendricks spent his two cents and winked. "You

and Mr. Diamond did me right, playing matchmaker for me and Leigh Anne. Won't be long before that bell's gonna chime at our wedding."

"You know I'll be delighted to help with the plans and reception. Leigh Anne will make a beautiful bride."

By the time Mr. Sibony stood before her, he eyed the jar. "Reckon I couldn't get two cents in that thing if I had to. Got another jar on hand?"

Rose gawked at the jar. She'd been so busy talking and blinking away emotional tears, she hadn't paid attention to the money jar. It was brimming!

"I'll take this jar over to the counters." Garret stepped up, switched jars, and gave her a lopsided grin. "Your sash is coming loose."

Rose reached around behind herself and fumbled with the wide bow Lacey insisted looked so chic over a bustle. "I'll be with you in a moment, Mr. Sneedly."

"Don't tie it too tight. You're always coming over to help when my kids get to wheezing and gasping from their croup. Last thing I want is you being breathless."

Mrs. Blanchard stopped by to say, "The quilt raffle brought in almost six dollars, and Cordelia says the cakewalk is coming up to nearly a dollar and a half now."

"How much more do we need for the bell? I can't see Leigh Anne's sign from here."

"I'll check on it."

Mr. Oates hefted his five-year-old twins and set them on the ledge. "Polly says she wants a kiss just as much as Peter does. Since I didn't see a sign that said otherwise, I figured you'd be one to bend a bit and take a peck from a girl."

Garret came by with a glass of lemonade for her. He raised

it and announced to the men still in line, "I'm making sure Rose keeps enough pucker power for all of you fellows."

She laughingly accepted the glass and took a quick sip. "Garret, I'm supposed to take Old Hannah to see the quilts. Who is supposed to take the booth now?"

"You're staying put. Mrs. Altwell showed her around, and now she's under the umbrella with Leigh Anne."

"Rose, are you playing mother hen again?" Reverend Jeffrey asked.

Rose gave him a startled look. She'd never imagined she'd have anyone line up to kiss her, but the pastor?

"I'm cutting in line. I need to get back over there so the mayor can come, too." He dropped a nickel into the jar and kissed her hand.

The banker chortled. "Now how am I supposed to follow a fine show like that?" He pulled a whole dollar from his pocket and put it in the jar.

Rose stared at it in utter astonishment.

He grabbed her glass, took a gulp, and carried it off without taking a kiss at all. He whistled a tune as he went, but Rose couldn't tell what it was because of the men's throaty laughter.

As the laughter died down, Leigh Anne let out a squeal. "We did it!"

The mayor stood by her and clapped his hands to get everyone's attention. "Ladies and gentlemen, I'm pleased to announce that the bazaar has been such a success; we've earned the money for the bell."

The banker turned around and stared at the nearly empty glass of lemonade. "What about the money in Rose's kissing jar?"

"I plan to add to it," Joel Creek called out as he stayed in line. "Schoolmarm's been saying she needs maps, and Mayor's been jawing about Buttonhole needing a library. I figure we'll find a good way to use it."

The bazaar continued. Folks started talking about what the extra money ought to buy. The line of men at the kissing booth shortened only because each man attending had bought a kiss—not a one had walked away. Garret came at the end.

He dropped two shiny new pennies in the jar and smiled. "Looks like I'm the last one."

She glanced around and lowered her voice to a mere whisper. "Looks like we won't have to plant that envelope, promising the Secret Giver will make up a shortfall."

"When you concocted that plan, you underestimated your appeal, Rose." Garret cupped her face in his hands. He studied her features slowly, one at a time. His gaze settled on her lips. "A man—especially this man—knows a beautiful woman when he sees her." He dipped his head.

Though flustered, Rose tilted her face up for the little peck. She expected the same friendly smooch she'd gotten from all of the other men. She puckered up a bit, but the minute their lips touched, there wasn't that little popping sound and Garret didn't pull away. Her head felt too heavy, her lids fluttered closed, and his lips stayed tenderly against hers. Everything inside of her melted.

Garret stood stock-still. He rested his forehead against hers and continued to hold her face in the chalice of his hands. "Rose, you are the sweetest woman God ever created."

She slowly opened her eyes and looked straight into his. This was her partner, her friend. He might not feel that overwhelming warmth and jumble of feelings, but she sure did. At the ripe age of twenty-five, she'd just had her first real kiss. She'd never imagined how it would make her knees tremble and her heart thunder. Suddenly, common sense washed over her. She and Garret had a pact. *Everything will be ruined if I let my heart fill up with utter nonsense.*

Panicked, she croaked, "Excuse me." She wheeled around and ran home.

eighteen

Garret drummed his fingers on the counter. He'd about lost patience. It was high time for Rose to stop acting silly. He'd seen the alarm in her eyes. The kiss he'd intended to be just a little touch of tenderness had given him away. She'd learned of his intentions sooner than he planned. Then, she'd run off like a scared rabbit.

For the past week, she'd been hiding, too. It irritated him, the way she avoided him. Instead of coming to the store to pray with him to seek God's guidance for the next Secret Giver project, she'd simply sent a note saying she'd support whatever he felt led to do.

Far too cunning for her own good, she'd come to shop for her eggs, butter, and milk when he had his afternoon off and Cordelia was minding the store.

To celebrate the successful bazaar, Mr. and Mrs. Milner invited him to supper. Mr. Milner happened to clear his throat, waggle his brows, and mention that the missus might have invited Rose. Garret intentionally waited ten minutes after he saw Rose pass by his window before he left. By the time he gained entry to the Milners', Rose already had knotted on an apron and was helping in the kitchen.

Garret didn't feel in the least bit sorry about the arrangement. She couldn't make a scene, take off her apron, and stomp home. He tried to make eye contact, but the silly woman refused to look at him. He consoled himself with the fact that when the evening wound down, he'd offer to escort her home, and simple manners would cause her to accept.

Biding his time never took so long.

The mantel clock chimed eight. Garret rose from the parlor chair and nodded to Mrs. Milner. "It's turning late. I thank you for a lovely meal." He shook Mr. Milner's hand. "Pleasant evening. Very pleasant. I'll be happy to escort Miss Masterson home."

Rose stood stiff as a tin soldier as he slipped her summer shawl about her shoulders. "Thank you." The words came out of her as if someone were squeezing her so tightly, she could barely whisper a syllable.

They stepped outside, and he tucked her hand into the bend of his arm. *Finally. Finally, I can talk some sense into this silly, lovable goose.*

"Rose?"

She turned toward the fence. "Yes, Sheriff?" Garret bit back a groan.

"Doc's tied up with a couple of dimwits who got into a brawl over at the saloon." The sheriff rested his hand on the chest-high green picket fence and buffed his badge with the other shirt cuff. "Sneedly's gone to Macon, and the missus is alone with her brood. She sent the oldest to see if you could help out. The kids are all croupy from the hay fever again."

❧

Rose twisted and wrestled to fasten the last button on her dress. That one between her shoulder blades never seemed to be so difficult before—*before Garret made sure I had all of those new dresses, skirts, and shirtwaists.* The completion of the thought made her ache. From the first day they'd met, her life had never been the same. It hadn't taken long for a comfortable friendship to develop between them. How could she have lost her senses and let one kiss turn her world upside down?

A glance in the mirror proved that the heat she felt showed in the form of a virulent blush. Even her drab, old brown paisley day gown didn't tame the effect of the color. Until she could regain and maintain her composure, she'd have to avoid Garret.

In the meantime, she'd been keeping busy. By filling every hour of her day with a chore, task, or deed, she actually managed to suppress the memory of that kiss—sometimes. Rose grabbed her hairbrush and started to untangle the snarls she'd gotten during another restless night. Somehow, the braid she normally wore to bed had come unraveled. Stroke after stroke, she tried to talk sense into herself. When she started to twist her hair, she knew forgetting Garret was an impossible task. Even this simple action brought back the time he'd pinned up her hair. She shivered at the memory.

Think of something—anything—to do today. I could bake. Pea—no, nothing peach. Definitely not a cobbler. I don't want him thinking I was trying to pander to his whims if he should stop by. He'd better not stop by. Why hasn't he stopped by? She shook her head. *I can't let that man drive me daft. Something else. I have to think of something else. . . . Apple. Yes, apple. Not a cobbler, either. A pie. There. That's a good idea. I could take it to share with Cordelia and her girls.*

Rose stuck in one last hairpin, then left her bedroom and headed straight for the kitchen. Tying on her apron, she frowned at the bowl in the center of her table. Three apples nestled in the center of it—shiny red apples. They were the wrong kind for baking, and there weren't enough of them even if she could have used them. She'd dehydrated apples aplenty, but the thought of making a dried apple pie in a season when fresh fruit abounded seemed ludicrous.

Bread. She could use a loaf, and the Sneedlys went through three loaves a day. With the children still sniffling and coughing, Lorna didn't have the time to bake. Rose grabbed her largest bowls and set to work.

A little less than two hours later, the yeasty smell of bread filled the kitchen. With the summer heat, the batches of dough rose far more quickly than usual. The first loaves were still in the oven, and the second batch would follow as soon as she took those out to cool. Rose had scoured the flour from her cutting board, mopped the floor, and washed the measuring cups, spoons, and bowls. She looked about for something to do.

Even in the few moments when she was between tasks, her mind whirled. *Why did Garret do that? Kiss me like that? We were supposed to be friends. How are we ever going to be friends again? He's a man of the world—how could he have risked our partnership, all for one meaningless kiss?*

She'd had dozens and dozens of kisses that day. Not a one of them made her feel anything more than neighborly warmth. Then Garret's kiss sparked something deep inside she'd never known existed. *He hasn't even tried to see me. The kiss meant nothing to him at all. For him, it was a two-cent donation. For me, it was everything. I have to stop thinking about it. I have to forget.*

The Sears catalogue caught her eye. Desperate for diversion, she pulled it from the shelf and set it on the table. Aaron Grim was in critical need of new clothes. Rose turned to the index, found the proper pages, and flipped to them.

What size would Aaron wear? She winced at the requirement of height, weight, and measurements.

If Garret were here, he'd know the right size.

"Nonsense," she said aloud. "I did just fine before he ever came. I'll do just fine on my own."

But we're partners. We've been praying, and God has been gracious to guide us.

"God blessed me long before I had a so-called partner," she muttered as she thumbed through the pages, waiting for something to catch her eye.

The women's clothing captured her attention. Cordelia hadn't had new clothes in ages. She was always busy sewing something for the girls since they were growing so fast. If Hugo was serious about courting her, Cordelia needed to have some pretty things to wear.

Why, I don't need to order anything from the catalogue. I can go to Lacey. She'd do such a nice job, and Cordelia could choose what she likes. We all had so much fun when we decided on the fabric and patterns for my clothes. I know! I can order some drawers and vests for her and the girls from the catalogue, and I can make one of those cut-and-paste letters and direct Lacey to make clothes for Cordelia.

Rose started to fill out an order form for the items. She could never provide for such needs with Garret present. This was all for the best. Oops. She'd written "best" instead of "vest."

She started the form over again, only to smell something burning. She jumped up from the table.

The edge of one of the loaves was singed—not badly. She could keep that one herself. Consoled by that thought, Rose stuck the second batch into the oven and went back to her catalogue.

She filled out all of the necessary information for fine,

pure Swiss ribbed, summer-weight silk vests and merrily ordered one in each color: black, salmon, apricot, white, and light blue. Vests for the girls were easy enough—all she needed to record were the girls' ages and the type of vests desired. Drawers for Cordelia; pantalets for the girls.

No, no, no. Rose crumpled the order form and tossed it into the stove. Cordelia was sure Zeb Hepplewhite was the Secret Giver. She'd be mortified if she thought for a second that a man had dared to buy lingerie for her and the girls.

That left clothes. Rose grabbed a *Gazette* and a blank sheet of paper. She had to hunt high and low before she recalled sticking her scissors in with her strips of bandaging after she'd had to patch up Prentice's knee the last time. Since she was out of paste, she made some with a dab of flour, a dash of salt, and a bit of water.

This was so much more fun by lantern light on the back porch with Garret.

The thought stopped her midsnip. Caramel meowed and jumped up into her lap. She started to purr loudly. Rose set down the shears and cradled the kitten in her arms. "Oh, Caramel, there's nothing worse than a lonely spinster pining for a love that was never meant to be."

≈

"I'd like to speak with you about something." Garret waited until Cordelia placed the last tin of Parlor Pride stove polish on the shelf and turned around.

The corners of her eyes crinkled. "It's about Rose, isn't it?"

He nodded. It occurred to him that he'd propped the doors wide open to allow a pleasant breeze to blow through, but he didn't want this conversation to become community gossip. No one was sitting on the benches, but he didn't want to take a chance, so he walked toward her. "I stopped over at her place again today, but she wasn't there. Talking sense into a woman might not be easy, but I don't have a fighting chance if I can't track her down!"

"I confess, I saw you kiss her."

Cordelia hadn't spoken loudly, but she'd not taken the hint to mute her tone, either. Mr. Deeter must have overheard her because he called out from behind the window, "Half of Buttonhole saw him kiss her. Whooo-ooo-ie!"

Cordelia had the grace to look chagrined that she hadn't been more mindful of the delicate nature of the conversation. She leaned a bit closer and murmured, "I have an inkling what kind of sense you aim to impart."

Garret didn't reply. He wasn't ashamed of his love, but he figured Rose ought to be the first woman he told.

Mr. Deeter called over, " 'Bout time you went and bought a ring 'stead of selling 'em, if you ask me."

As he chuckled at his clever opinion, Cordelia coughed to muffle her laugh. Garret drummed his fingers on the closest shelf. "That's what I need to talk to you about. Could you give me an estimate of Rose's ring size?"

Cordelia perked up and bustled over to the locked jewelry case. "She's a five. I'm positive she's a five. She loaned me some of her gloves last Easter. Glove and ring size are the same, you know."

Garret sauntered over to the case. "See anything in there you think is pretty?"

"She was looking through her catalogue just a few weeks before the bazaar and asked me the very same question. That one on the far left with the little swirls is similar to the ring we both decided was the prettiest."

"Hmmm. Would you mind trying it on?"

A minute later, Garret slid the ring on Cordelia's finger. "Oh, Garret, it's beautiful."

Mr. Deeter cleared his throat, but it didn't cover the gasp.

Garret glanced over and saw Mrs. Jeffrey and Rose in the doorway to the store. Mrs. Jeffrey grabbed Rose by the arm and yanked her off the stoop. Garret raced for the door. "Rose!"

The women were across the street, and two wagons traveled the normally quiet road in opposite directions. By the time they passed, Rose was gone.

nineteen

"You should stay here for the night." Mrs. Jeffrey patted Rose's arm. "After such a disquieting event, it's not right for a body to be alone. The bed in the spare room is all made up, and you can borrow a nightgown."

Rose set her knife and fork across her plate. She'd forced herself to eat two bites of each dish her hostess had served. Every last one of them got stuck halfway down, and now the food sat like a cannonball in her stomach.

Reverend Jeffrey muttered something about a deacons' meeting and excused himself. As he passed by Rose's chair, he patted her shoulder. "Romans 8:28 says, 'And we know that all things work together for good to them that love God, to them who are the called according to his purpose.' This trial has already been through the heavenly Throne Room. We'll keep you in prayer and have faith that this will turn out according to God's will."

She nodded. He was right, but it still hurt. After she helped do the supper dishes, Rose wanted to be alone. "Thank you for the solace of your company today. I truly appreciate it, but I need to go home now. Caramel—my kitten—needs to be fed."

Bless her heart, Mrs. Jeffrey didn't argue. "Okay, Dear. After you feed her, if you decide you'd like to come back here, the door is open, and you're more than welcome."

"Thank you." Rose slipped out the back door and went

home. Once there, she started heating water for a bath and sat down to read her Bible. The faded, plum-colored ribbon marked where she'd left off yesterday in the fourth chapter of 1 Peter. Verses 12 and 13 leapt off the page at her: "Beloved, think it not strange concerning the fiery trial which is to try you, as though some strange thing happened unto you: But rejoice, inasmuch as ye are partakers of Christ's sufferings; that, when his glory shall be revealed, ye may be glad also with exceeding joy." Suddenly, common sense washed over her.

She stared at the words. "Lord, it is strange. I don't understand why this is happening. I thought Hugo and Cordelia were falling in love, and I was so happy for them. It was bad enough when I thought Garret didn't return my feelings, but for him to be betrothed to Cordelia—it just makes my heart ache. It's so selfish of me. I should be thrilled for them, but all I feel is so lonely and empty. Was this part of Christ's suffering? To be single and watch others find the contentment of love and marriage? Until now, there's never been anyone who stirred my heart. Now, my heart is breaking. I don't know what glory there is for You in this. I don't see any joy in it. Help me to understand, Father."

❧

Garret gave Cordelia some of the new Bayer headache powder from Germany. She'd managed to weep herself into a migraine, and Mr. Deeter kindly walked her home after leaving the post office in the hands of Percy Watkins, the postman, who had finished his deliveries for the day.

Garret didn't care about keeping the store open; he wanted to track down Rose and explain matters. In just those few seconds he'd seen her, her beautiful green eyes had gone huge with shock, and her face—her pretty face—turned white as the wicker basket she usually carried.

He hadn't had a chance to get to Rose. Mrs. Blanchard plowed in like a yacht under full sail. She'd not come alone, either. Mrs. Busby and Leigh Anne's grandmother were in her wake. Mrs. Blanchard stabbed him in the chest with her forefinger to accentuate her words. "How dare you upset our Rose!"

"I didn't—"

"You most certainly did, young man. I heard it from an eyewitness. Bad enough you did it at all, but in front of that poor child!"

"What? Now wait a minute."

"Don't you deny it. Poor little Prentice saw and heard it all. You've been an utter cad, and we will not stand for it, will we, girls?"

"No. Never," Mrs. Busby hastened to agree.

Leigh Anne's grandmother edged around and squinted at him. "I expected better of you. You're no green-behind-the-ears boy; you're a grown man. There's no excuse for dallying with a woman's affections—especially someone as sensitive as Rose Masterson."

"I agree." His quiet, confident words didn't register. The women had come to speak their minds, and he figured he might as well let them. It would take less time than trying to defend himself. Mrs. Kiersty came in, caught the drift of the conversation, and gave him a heated look that could have boiled an egg.

"Hugo and Cordelia belong together. They both have children. I've been coaxing them into each other's arms ever since Christmas, and if you've ruined it for them and those darling little children, I'll never buy so much as a grain of salt in this store again," Mrs. Kiersty announced.

"You'd be bored to distraction with any of the demure younger girls." Mrs. Blanchard gave up poking him in the chest—she jabbed at his arm instead. "Oh, I admit, I wanted you to sweep my Constance off her feet. It didn't take long for me to realize the two of you simply wouldn't suit. You need a woman of Rose's spunk."

"Amen." He nodded.

"It's not fair to judge her by her ramshackle appearance," Mrs. Busby quavered tearfully. "Her apron might be smudged, but it's because she's always cooking for someone or minding a child to help out."

"She has a gentle touch," he said softly.

"God looks on the heart, young man," Mrs. Lula Mae Evert declared.

"I'm glad He does, and Rose has the purest heart of anyone I've ever met; but I'm a man, and I'm more than pleased to look at her outward appearance. She's a charming woman."

"Well, then, if that's not your problem, then let me say, time was, I felt scandalized at her willy-nilly, disorganized ways." Mrs. Sowell tapped him on the chest with the handle of her parasol. "But Rose's house would look neat as a pin if she wasn't always off, helping someone else."

"Because she dusts for Mrs. Sneedly and washes Old Hannah's windows?" Garret held his ground. "Or because she spends all sorts of time minding her herb garden so Doc has curatives for folks?"

The women fell silent and exchanged baffled looks. Garret folded his arms akimbo. "You ladies don't need to champion Rose Masterson. I already have my heart set on her, but I had hoped to tell her so before the rest of the community knew."

"Then why did you give Cordelia a ring?"

"Cordelia was just trying on a ring so I could get the right size for Rose."

"Boy, do you all look like a flock of gossiping hens." Percy Watkins smirked from the post office.

"You all love Rose and were protecting her," Garret said diplomatically. "You've been her family, and I appreciate how you rushed to defend her. It does my heart good to see you all care for her so much, and as soon as I can declare my love *to* her instead of telling it to half of Buttonhole, we'll all celebrate. Now if you'll excuse me, I need some quiet time to pray and decide how to unravel this mess."

"I could go to her," Mrs. Kiersty offered.

"I'll handle this myself." His tone brooked no argument.

Garret fasted from his evening meal and prayed instead. Shortly thereafter, he headed toward Rose's house. A single light shone in the kitchen, but that proved she was home and awake, so he knocked on her door.

Rose barely opened the door a crack. Her nose was red, and her eyes held an ache that made his heart twist. She said nothing at all.

"Rose, we need to talk."

She shook her head.

Garret pushed the door open a bit farther. "Rosie—"

"I'm having my devotions."

"Come out on the veranda, and we'll share them. We haven't prayed together for a week and a half."

"No. Good-bye, Mr. Diamond."

"Garret. My name is Garret."

She tried to shut the door, but he wouldn't let her. Instead of struggling, she walked away. He could see her pick up her Bible and carry the lamp to the back part of the house.

Garret intentionally left the door open. He crossed the street, spoke with Hugo, then came back with a big washtub and a shovel. The moonlight and street gaslight fixture illuminated Rose's yard quite adequately. He went to the fence and started to work. The shovel bit into the ground.

"Garret Diamond, you stop that this very minute!"

twenty

Rose stood in her doorway and stared at him in horror. It had taken every shred of her resolve and faith not to fall apart when he came to the door. Tears burned behind her eyes, and her nose tingled with suppressed emotion, but she'd managed to be civil and tell him to leave. Barely. She'd wanted to run away from him; she'd wanted to throw herself into his arms. Honor and dignity forced her to turn and walk away. The sound of digging in her yard brought her back, though.

"Quit that!"

He ignored her. A hefty swoop, and the shovel bit the earth. He stomped on it a few times, wiggled and removed the shovel, only to repeat the action in the dirt just inches to the right.

Rose ran out and grabbed his arm. Anger gave her strength. "Stop this. You can't do it. You can't. I won't let you."

"You already gave me permission."

Affronted at his galling lie, she shot back, "I most certainly did not!"

"I have the note you sent me. You gave me permission to do whatever I felt was appropriate for the Secret Giver. You even said you'd be a full partner. Well, Partner, you're donating these plants, and I'm giving my strength."

"You're not giving; you're taking away. You know how much these mean to Cordelia. Destroying them won't erase her memories of Jonathan. Don't do this. It'll hurt her."

Garret forced the shovel into the earth yet again, but he let go of the handle and wiped his hands on the sides of his trousers. "Cordelia is like a sister to me, Rose."

She wanted to believe him, but he'd given her every reason not to. She'd seen him place that ring on Cordelia's finger. Rose looked at him in silence. Meeting his eyes was almost impossible.

His hands cupped her face—just the way they had when he'd kissed her. A cry tore from her chest as she tried to jerk away, but he didn't let go.

"Rose, it's you I love. Didn't my kiss tell you that back at the bazaar?"

"That kiss," she whispered brokenly, "was nothing more than a moment of madness."

"Then I'm headed for a lifetime of insanity, because I'm counting on marrying you."

"You can't mean that. I saw you put that ring on Cordelia's finger, and she was thrilled. She said it was beautiful."

"I had two ulterior motives. Hugo asked me to see if there was a special ring she liked. Yes, he aims to propose."

Rose could barely understand what he said. Everything was so mixed up. A confused mind and an aching heart were a deadly combination.

"That's why I'm digging up the bindweed, Rosie. We're going to transplant it over to Hugo's yard. It's his way of letting Cordelia keep a bit of her past while making new memories with him."

"Oh, Garret—that is so precious!" *How wonderful it is for Cordelia to have a man love her like that.* With her next breath, Rose couldn't stop the purely selfish thought, *But why can't Garret love me with that same kind of burning devotion?*

"Hugo and Cordelia's courtship isn't the most important thing happening. Listen to me, Rose. The main reason I had Cordelia try on a ring was so I knew what size to get for you." He slipped his hand into a pocket and withdrew an ornate band with a sparkling diamond. "Rose Masterson, I'm head over heels in love with you. Marry me. I need you in my life—you're already in my heart. Be my helpmeet, my wife."

Her breath caught. She wanted to say yes so badly. Oh, how she wanted to. Instead, she forced herself to whisper, "You know nothing about me."

"I know all I need to know. You have a heart as big as heaven."

"I—I'm different. I can't keep my gloves or apron spotless, and my hair's always a fright. I'm not supposed to know it, but they call me and my house ramshackle. Did you know that?"

With his thumb, Garret brushed away the single tear she hadn't managed to blink away. He slowly, tenderly twirled his forefinger so some of her escaped wisps of hair curled into a ringlet by her left temple. The action made her weak in the knees.

"You're perfect the way you are, Rose. Your beauty is in how you don't fuss with the details and how you radiate with joy over everything. Your gloves are smudged because you hug grubby little boys who don't have a mother. Your apron is smeared because you cook and bake and cut flowers for others. Those aren't flaws, Sweetheart. They're badges of love."

"You're just trying to be honorable. Of course you want a woman who is young and pretty and—"

Garret shook his head. He gazed at her steadily. "There are young women in town, and they're pretty in their own ways, but to me, they're all pretty boring, too. I want a woman with spirit and depth. I've fallen in love with a woman who is every bit as beautiful on the inside as she is on the out. I want you, Rose."

"But you don't know." The anguish she felt rang in her words.

He rested his forehead against hers as he invited, "Then tell me. Whatever it is, we'll work through it. I don't for a second believe God would give me this love for you if He wouldn't also give us strength to overcome any obstacle in our path."

"Could we sit down?"

"Sure, Sweetheart." He walked her to the veranda and sat beside her on the small oak bench.

Rose steeled herself for what was to come. The lawyer hadn't spared her feelings when he'd explained her financial status. *There are two kinds of men—those who will want to marry you because of your money and those who won't want anything to do with you because you'll unman them when they discover you could buy and sell them a thousand times over.*

Garret crooked a finger under her chin and turned her face up toward his. "Folks here assumed you're an orphan and were never married. Is that right?"

"I've never been married. For that matter, my daddy never approved of anyone who came calling, so I've never been courted." She felt heat scorch her cheeks. "Until the bazaar, I'd never been kissed."

"There's only one man who's ever going to kiss you again, Rose. I'm that man."

Raw possession rang in his tone. Instead of feeling afraid, it actually calmed her and gave her the courage to tell him a little more.

"Daddy's business necessitated a move to Georgia, so when he and Mama passed on, I was essentially on my own." When Garret didn't respond and continued to wait for her to say more, Rose tried to ease into the topic as carefully as she could. "I do have an aunt up in Boston. Other than that, Buttonhole is my family."

"Before the war," Garret responded, "my family was in the shipping business—the Newcombs. I have a few distant cousins in Boston. What's your aunt's last name?"

She couldn't hold his gaze. Her focus shifted downward.

"Rose," he asked very slowly, "is your last name really Masterson?"

After a prolonged silence, she grudgingly admitted, "It's Masterson-Cardiff. I chose to shorten it when I moved here." She glanced up to see how he was reacting to that news.

Garret stared at her for a long moment, then shook his head in disbelief. "You're the heiress of the Cardiff rail-road fortune? Rose, you could travel the world and live in luxury, yet you choose to live in Buttonhole, Virginia?"

She pulled away from his touch. "It's where I'm happy." She braced herself for his reaction. He was too generous and honorable to be a greedy fortune hunter. That meant he was going to decide they were unsuitable matches, after all.

Garret stretched his long legs out, cupped his hands behind his neck, and leaned his head back. The whole bench shook with his deep, throaty chuckle.

That was the last reaction she'd expected from him. Rose twisted on the bench and demanded, "Just what is so hilarious?"

"I was just thinking how much fun we're going to have. Sweetheart, the emporium is booming. I've made more of a profit in three months than the previous owner made in a year and a half. We can live very comfortably on what I make, and we can use the rest to play Secret Giver from now until the cows come home."

Rose stared at him in astonishment. He didn't care. He honestly didn't care that she had money or that tidiness eluded her. Then something in his expression shifted. Her heart skipped a beat.

"As long as we're trading secrets, there's something you ought to know."

She gulped, then lifted her chin. He'd had faith and love enough to stand by her. Well, she had faith and love enough to do the same for him. "You said with God's help, we'd make it through whatever obstacles lay in our path."

He let out a big sigh. "Rose, I'm just going to say it straight out."

She mentally braced herself for whatever dreadful information he needed to share.

"I hate peaches."

She blinked at him in utter amazement. "You hate peaches? Is that all?"

He shrugged. "Well, I've tried every trick in the book to be with you, and I've managed to avoid eating your peach stuff most of the time. I just can't imagine you spending all of that time and energy to make me peach cobbler when I'd rather have something else."

"What else would you like?"

His large, warm hand cupped the back of her neck as he leaned closer. "Your kisses are all the dessert I ever want or need." His breath washed over her, and Rose shivered at the delicious thrill of knowing he loved her. "Tell me you'll marry me," he said.

She scooted closer. "I love you, Garret. I'd be honored to be your wife."

"Then I'm ready for some dessert." He kissed her until her toes curled in her shoes, then slipped the ring on her finger.

⁂

Four weeks later, Rose wore her mother's wedding gown. Cordelia was the matron of honor, and Hugo served as best man. Proud as could be, Zeb Hepplewhite walked Rose down the aisle to Wagner's "Wedding March"—played on the harmonica by Prentice.

No one mentioned that the bride's gloves had a smudge or that the groom's cuff links didn't match. Somehow, it just seemed right. Mrs. Jeffrey and Cordelia had spent half the morning and an entire card of hairpins to anchor Rose's hair and veil into place. Zeb decided he needed a peck on the cheek before he gave her away, and the veil tilted a bit to the back while her hair shifted to the right.

"Would you like my wife to help fix you?" Reverend Jeffrey whispered.

Garret shook his head and took Rose's hand. "This is my girl. She doesn't need to be fixed because she's just right the way she is."

"Hair looks like Miss Rose, now," Prentice said as he shoved his harmonica in the pocket of his new pants. "But are you sure that's who's under all of that?"

Garret raised his brows. Reverend Jeffrey shrugged, and Rose laughingly nodded. Garret lifted the veil and told her, "I have a feeling we're not going to always follow convention, but we'll always follow Christ and live in love."

They said their vows and sealed them with a kiss. The church's new bell pealed for the first time to celebrate the marriage, and the newlyweds went off to honeymoon in an undisclosed location.

Two months later, Mr. and Mrs. Garret Diamond returned from their honeymoon. Rose gasped as they drew up to the house. Gone was her old, tilted, peeling fence. In its place was a beautiful white picket fence. Someone had planted yellow climbing roses along it.

A fresh coat of paint covered the house, the gardens were all weeded, and the inside of the house was spic and span. No one admitted to having any part in these projects. Mr. Deeter shoved his hands in his pockets and said, "God's the source of everything. Folks 'round here know it."

Lula Mae nodded. "I guess maybe we all have a bit of the Secret Giver in us if we follow that Bible verse about giving without one hand knowing what the other's doing."

Garret nestled Rose close to his side. She smiled up at him. After they'd visited Niagara Falls and the Statue of Liberty, he'd surprised her with a trip to Chicago. They'd spent two days wandering through the huge Sears, Roebuck, and Company warehouse that was crammed with possibilities.

Now as they stood with their friends, Garret wondered what Rose would think when all of the books he'd ordered for a town library arrived. And as she gazed at the young rosebushes, Rose wondered what Garret would do this evening when she told him about the baby.

A Letter To Our Readers

Dear Reader:

In order that we might better contribute to your reading enjoyment, we would appreciate your taking a few minutes to respond to the following questions. We welcome your comments and read each form and letter we receive. When completed, please return to the following:

Fiction Editor
Heartsong Presents
PO Box 719
Uhrichsville, Ohio 44683

1. Did you enjoy reading *Ramshakle Rose* by Cathy Marie Hake?
   ❏ Very much! I would like to see more books by this author!
   ❏ Moderately. I would have enjoyed it more if

   _____

   _____

   _____

2. Are you a member of Heartsong Presents? ❏ Yes ❏ No
   If no, where did you purchase this book? _____

   _____

3. How would you rate, on a scale from 1 (poor) to 5 (superior), the cover design? _____

4. On a scale from 1 (poor) to 10 (superior), please rate the following elements.

   ____ Heroine   ____ Plot
   ____ Hero   ____ Inspirational theme
   ____ Setting   ____ Secondary characters

5. These characters were special because?_____
_____
_____

6. How has this book inspired your life?_____
_____
_____

7. What settings would you like to see covered in future
   Heartsong Presents books? _____
_____
_____

8. What are some inspirational themes you would like to see
   treated in future books? _____
_____
_____

9. Would you be interested in reading other Heartsong
   Presents titles? ❏ Yes ❏ No

10. Please check your age range:
        ❏ Under 18   ❏ 18-24
        ❏ 25-34   ❏ 35-45
        ❏ 46-55   ❏ Over 55

Name_____
Occupation _____
Address _____
City_____ State_____ Zip_____

Heart♥ong

HISTORICAL ROMANCE IS CHEAPER BY THE DOZEN!

Any 12
Heartsong
Presents titles
for only
$30.00*

Buy any assortment of twelve *Heartsong Presents* titles and save 25% off of the already discounted price of $3.25 each!

*plus $2.00 shipping and handling per order and sales tax where applicable.

HEARTSONG PRESENTS TITLES AVAILABLE NOW:

(If ordering from this page, please remember to include it with the order form.)